Club Silken
Come Hard Book 1

COPYRIGHT © 2020 by Jerrie Alexander
Publisher: Jerrie Alexander

Cover illustrator: Brynna Curry
Brynna@BrynnaCurry.com
Edits by: Eve Arroyo
www.evearroyo.com[1]

Acknowledgments

Kym Roberts, I appreciate all your support and encouragement. I also appreciate your keen eye and honest opinions.

Brynna Curry, thank you for your talent and patience and for designing my beautiful book covers.

Julie Cupp, with the Formatting Faries, your knowledge and patience are invaluable.

This is a work of fiction. Names, characters, places, and incidents are either the product of the author's imagination or are used fictitiously, and the resemblance to actual persons living or dead, business establishments, events, or locales is entirely coincidental and not intended by the author.

Published in the United States of America

Come Hard is book 1 of the Club Silken Series. Each book is written as a standalone story with a guaranteed happy ending. No cliffhangers.

This series is intended for mature audiences only due to sexual situations, explicit language, and some BDSM.

COME HARD
Book 1 of the Club Silken Series

Chapter 1

Morgan

My alcohol sedated brain barely registers the distant buzzing of my phone. I run my hand over the table next to my bed and come up empty. Where the hell is my cell? I open one eye and focus on the clock. My heart slams into my chest; good news never comes at three in the morning.

I cram my feet into the bunny slippers Nana gave me for Christmas last year, and run to the living room. My purse is next to my front door, right where I kicked off my heels the minute I got home two hours ago.

Leaning down to open my bag, the earthquake in my head increases tenfold. My stomach teeters on the edge of upheaval, a combination of too many daiquiris and fear. I dump everything out of my purse onto the carpet. Oh, hell no, my phone is inside my bag but my wallet isn't. The thought of someone buying a big-screen television using my credit cards makes me want to throw up. I pull up my phone message while trying to remember the last time I used my wallet at the bar.

"This call is for Morgan Kimball." The male voice is deep and raspy like he'd just taken a shot of whiskey. "Your billfold was found by the cleanup crew at Gloss Nightclub." A wave of relief hits me. "We open tomorrow at one p.m., or, if you want to pick it up tonight, we'll be here until around four."

"I can't wait until tomorrow afternoon," I mutter. There's no heavy traffic this time of morning and I can be at the club in twenty minutes. I rush to the bathroom, take two aspirin, finger comb my hair into a scrunchy, and slip on a knee-length sweater to cover my tank top and boy shorts.

I hurry to the parking lot and within minutes I'm driving down the interstate, constantly glancing at my speedometer to make sure I'm not speeding. I'll never get to the club on time if I have to explain to a policeman why I'm out in the wee hours of the morning wearing my pj's.

I park in front of Gloss with ten minutes to spare and rush to the door. "Hello," I call out while knocking loud enough to get someone's attention. This part of the city isn't residential so I pound a little harder. "Hello. My name is Morgan Kimball and I'm here to pick up my wallet."

The huge wooden door opens slowly, and an older, grey-haired man greets me with a smile. The corners of his eyes are crinkled and the laugh lines around his mouth give him a friendly look. I like him immediately.

"Come inside. I'll get it for you." He closes and locks the door behind us. I stop and arch an eyebrow. "You're safe here. We just don't want any strays coming in."

"I understand." I glance around the club. The inside looks different now that the bright, overhead lights are on. The club seems to be a large and lonely open space when a few hours ago it was alive with people, and the walls were vibrating with music. The stage that held the band is dark, with black sheets thrown over the instruments. I'm startled when a second male voice joins us.

"Mr. Henry, I'll finish up here. You can go home."

I look up and see the man whose voice is sending hot streaks across my skin. It's the same deep, throaty voice that left the message on my voicemail. The man, wearing a black T-shirt, black slacks, and a sexy grin, is standing at the end of the long marble bar. He has a yellow rubber glove on one hand and a white bucket in the other. Tall with broad shoulders, his dark eyes scorch my body from head to toe.

"Join me?" He cocks his head and waits.

Between his looks and voice, a sudden need rushes across my skin and moisture dampens my panties. I'm not sure I can make my feet move from just inside the door. Maybe, Mr. Henry needs to stay.

Mr. Henry smiles again. "Thanks, boss."

"Drive safely." Mr. Sexy doesn't take his eyes off me.

"Good night." The older gentleman nods at me and then disappears down a hallway. I hear a door creak and then slam closed.

A tingle runs up my spine. Mr. Sexy and I are alone. We stare at each other for a long moment, and the temperature in the bar seems to rise before I find my voice. "My wallet?"

"I'll get it for you." He sets the glove and bucket down, walks behind the bar, retrieves my wallet from under the counter, and then closes the distance between us. His stride is confident, like a man who knows exactly where he's going and what he wants. My heart flutters at the way his T-shirt hugs his body, outlining his thick chest and tapered waist. Mr. Sexy is built like Mr. Clean but he doesn't smell like any cleaning solution I've ever used. His scent is earthy and fresh and so damned enticing.

"And you are?" I ask.

"Zackary Pierce. Zack to you." He hangs onto my billfold but holds out his other hand, and for some reason, I take it. His skin is warm, and his fingers intertwine with mine. His thumb brushes across my wrist, sending heat rippling up my arm.

"Zack," I say slowly. "I appreciate that someone found my wallet. Losing it would've been a pain in my ass." This guy is drop-dead gorgeous, and my brain tells me to leave, but my feet seem rooted to the floor.

"The cleanup crew found it under one of the tables." Zack leads me to the bar, pulls out a stool, and pats the seat. "There's stale coffee, but I recommend a drink."

I shake my head, wondering if anybody ever tells him no. "It's late."

He smiles, stunning me with gorgeous, white teeth and a dimple on his right cheek. "One Baileys Irish Cream to finish off the night."

My resistance vaporizes. "You found my weakness." I slide onto the seat, aware of the smooth hardwood under me. "One Baileys."

His dark gaze locks with mine as he walks behind the bar and pours two Baileys. He hands one to me and lifts his glass toward me. "To new friends."

"Absolutely." I touch my glass to his. "I don't usually go out on Thursday night, but I admit this has been an interesting evening."

Zack joins me, pulls out a stool, and sits facing me. His thick, dark hair is slightly mussed and just long enough to brush the top of his collar. Who is this guy and why are my hormones zinging around my system?

"You don't go out on a work night?"

"Not normally, but it's Independence Day weekend. I have a three day weekend."

"Here's to long weekends." He lifts his drink to his mouth and takes a sip. His tongue slips out and slides across his lips. "My God, you're a beautiful creature."

"I am not," I scoff and roll my eyes. "I'm not wearing makeup and I'm in my pj's."

"Are you now?" Zack reaches out with his index finger and slides my sweater off my shoulder. My nipples immediately harden. I jerk it back in place, covering myself. "Damn, you're crazy."

He moans then looks up at me with dark, lust-filled eyes. "I've been called a lot of things, but never crazy."

"What do they call you?"

"Dominant, possessive, blunt, and some even call me Sir."

"I need to go home." I start to slide off the stool, but his hand on my knee stops me.

"Don't." He clears his throat. "I like looking at you. You're fucking stunning."

Completely at a loss for words, I swallow. My breasts are heavy, full, in need of caressing. "Right."

"Would you believe your footwear won me over?" He chuckles as if he's trying to lighten the mood.

Immediately, I find my voice. "Hey, these slippers were the last gift I received from my Nana."

Zack's face softens. "She was important to you. Tell me about her."

"I don't know you well enough to share the story. Look, I'm not into one-night stands. I've had a couple and they never turn out well."

"It's okay. You don't have to tell me about the shoes." His grin spreads, flashing his dimple. "Let's get to know each other first."

This whole scene is insane, and I can't hold back any longer. I throw my head back and laugh. "I have to go before I decide we're both crazy."

Zack tilts his head and studies my face. My strength weakens when he leans closer and his scent wraps around me. The man oozes sex. The heat from his body pulls me toward him. I reached for my billfold, but he catches my hand, turns it palm up, and starts stroking my skin with his thumb again.

I pull my hand free and lift my glass to my lips. In a very unladylike move, I gulp down the rest of my Baileys. A slight smile lifts his lush lips as he watches me try to control my trembling hands. "Thanks for the drink and rescuing my wallet."

Sex with a stranger isn't on my to-do list, but Zack is so tempting I consider making an exception. But . . . leaving is a better idea so I push my stool back and stand. Zack walks to the exit with me, reaching around to open the door. I almost tell him I feel like I just auditioned for a B movie.

"I'd like to see you again." His breath is warm, disturbing a lock of my hair falling from my messy ponytail.

I don't take that last step outside. Instead, I freeze, admitting I want to see this through. My body reacts differently to him. It's as if he controls it, not me. As if he's the reason my nipples have pebbled. He's at least six foot-two and towers over my five-foot-five frame, and I hope he can't see my reaction to his nearness. "How did I not notice you when I was here earlier?"

"My partner took the night off. I came in to close up for him."

I turn to face him. "So, Zack Pierce, besides cleaning bars, what do you do for a living?"

"I own a brokerage firm." Zack tucks that loose strand of hair behind my ear.

"And you're partners in Gloss?"

"I'm co-owner of three nightclubs, Gloss, Gallants, and Club Silken. Club Silken is invitation only, and it's my responsibility."

"Invitation only? Do you mean a strip club?

"Not at all. It's a members-only club, a safe haven for adults to enjoy physical, psychological, and sexual role play. All participation is consensual, and the rules are followed. Our clientele dress code fluctuates from fully clothed to various stages of undress, but there's no pole dancing."

"Oh." I take a minute to digest everything he said, and my stomach bottoms out as I realize what he's described. "It's a BDSM club."

"Not just BDSM. It's a place where members can experience their sexual desires with complete assurance of privacy. Couples attend, but single members are allowed too. It gives them the opportunity to mingle and perhaps find someone to play with for the night. We're open Thursday, Friday, and Saturday from eight p.m. until four in the morning. Sunday we shutdown at midnight."

"Wow." It's the only response I can come up with. I'm too caught up in a fantasy about what goes on in his club and I find myself fascinated.

"Let me take you to dinner tomorrow night. If you're interested, I'll tell you more about the club."

A warm tingle starts at the base of my spine, streaking straight to the apex of my thighs. I want to clamp them together but don't. I've heard and read about adult clubs and some of the things that happen there. "I'm curious, but not convinced I'm interested."

"No one will pressure you to do anything. It's strictly your decision." Zack pauses, giving me time to think. "What do you say?"

My brain is screaming caution but my wet panties refuse to be denied. I want to see him again and I want to experience this man in his club. "I'd like that. You have my number."

"You can count on my call tomorrow." His gaze locks with mine.

"Good, I'll talk to you then."

"Drive safely."

I step outside, and he catches my elbow, walking me to my car. He opens the door while I stare up at him, wondering if he'll try to kiss me. God, how I want to taste his lips on mine. "Good night, Zack."

He cups my face with his hands, leans down, and covers my mouth with a soft kiss. Nothing too demanding, yet, somehow, filled with a promise of what's to come. "I need to warn you, I don't do permanent, but I don't like one-night stands either," he whispers against my lips. "Will you still take my call?"

"Yes." The word slips from my mouth before I can register what he said. *He doesn't do permanent.*

I drive away in total confusion. It's been a long time since a man, much less a stranger, had such a strong effect on my body. When he shoved my sweater off my shoulder and blatantly looked at my tits with lust in his eyes, my core tightened with desire. Maybe I'm glad I didn't slip on a bra before leaving home.

Zack is exciting, gorgeous, and not just a little intimidating. My hands don't stop shaking until I'm inside my apartment.

The past few years, my focus has been on pulling my life together. Since losing Nana, I have no one—well, a couple of terrific friends, but no family.

I try and fail to remember the last time I had sex. Well, good sex. The last man I dated started out being a great guy, but by the end of the first month, Dale had become bossy and demanding. He said I didn't dress right, my hair wasn't styled to his satisfaction, I didn't eat oysters, and my friends were beneath him. When he started demeaning Chels and Kayla, I ended the relationship. The last thing he said to me was that I was a lousy fuck. He put a hell of a dent in my self-confidence, and I'm still working to get past it. Going to Club Silken might be precisely what I need.

Chels and I celebrated Dale's exit with a bottle of wine and a romance movie. Chelsea Coffman and I have been friends since I joined the Slater Advertising Firm as an administrative assistant to the VP of Accounting. I'd been hired from the outside, and a handful of workers had expected someone from the inside to be selected. Admin for the Human Resources Director, Chels, was the first person in the company to truly welcome me. She introduced me to Kayla who works in payroll and is the perfect addition to our little group. Within a year, the two of us lived in the same apartment complex as Chels.

I'm dying to call Chels and tell her about Zack, but she'll kill me if I wake her this early. I hang up my sweater, kick off my slippers, and climb between the sheets for a few minutes of sleep. I doze off, hoping the promise in Zack's kiss isn't a fantasy.

****

Zack

I watch until her car is out of sight before adjusting my dick. I've been semi-erect since she walked in the door, but the intake of Morgan's breath and the desire in her eyes, after I kissed her, has my dick hard as stone and painfully wedged against my underwear. I go back inside, lock up, and head home, still shifting in my seat, searching for a comfortable position. Trying to convince my cock he isn't getting laid tonight isn't working.

Morgan's exactly the type of woman I enjoy introducing to the lifestyle. Taking her to dinner before telling her more about Club Silken gives me the opportunity to test her interest.

It's been a long time since I took a woman on a date. There are always women at the club looking for a quick, hard fuck, and I'm happy to oblige.

I try to push Morgan away from my thoughts by rehashing tonight's attendance. Gloss has been profitable from the beginning. Positioned in a well-traveled area of Chicago, the property set us back a bundle, but the bar has quickly become the hot place for business people to come after work. After happy hour, a band starts playing, and we often have standing room only. Tomorrow, I'll learn how the other two clubs fared tonight.

I pull into my underground parking garage and guide my Porsche into its assigned slot. I bypass the elevator, walk around to the lobby of my high rise, and scan my card to enter. The night watchman, Sidney, has been working here since I bought the penthouse three years ago and he looks forward to me checking in occasionally. No matter the hour, and it's five in the morning now, he always greets me the same way. "Good morning, Mr. Pierce. Did you have a good evening?"

"Morning, Sidney." Tall, thin, and very stoic, he knows all the residents by name. No visitor goes up the elevator without his permission from the owner. "The night was good, but the morning was better."

"I thought I spotted a hint of a smile on your face, Mr. Pierce." Sidney waggles his eyebrows.

"My name's Zack, by the way," I tell him for the hundredth time. He's at least thirty years older than me, and I wish he'd drop the Mister. "How's the family?"

"Sid Junior was accepted at Chicago University." Sidney's pride shows in his smile.

"Congratulations," I say, making a mental note to give his son a graduation present.

"Thanks." Sidney walks with me to the elevator and scans his card to enter the penthouse. "Get some rest, Mr. Pierce. The hours you work must be hard on the body."

The doors slide closed before I remind him to call me Zack again. I'm not into formal behavior; he works and earns his living just like I do.

The elevator opens into my living room, and I breathe in the quiet. It's dark inside, but I don't turn on the lights. I push the remote, and the drapes slide back, illuminating the room with Chicago's city lights. I drop my keys in a bowl next to the couch and then undress as I move to my bathroom.

I hit the shower with the mental image of Morgan's gorgeous curves, porcelain skin, and long, dark hair spread across my pillow. Under the spray of water, I press one hand against the shower wall and take my aching cock in my hand. I use my fist as a jackhammer and pound myself. It doesn't take long until I paint the shower walls with streams of cum. I dry off, brush my teeth, and crawl into bed.

Sleep doesn't come easy. Thoughts of Morgan won't give me a minute's rest. She has no idea how fucking hot she is, and I want to be the one who shows her. When I pushed her sweater off her shoulder and her nipples peaked and pushed against her tank top, I was hooked. Morgan intrigues the hell out of me. I finally fall asleep thinking about how her breasts will fit perfectly in my palms.

The smell of coffee and the sound of a vacuum cleaner drag me from an X-rated dream where Morgan is deep-throating my cock. I get up and pull on a pair of jogging shorts and a T-shirt before wandering into the kitchen. I pour myself a cup and lean against the counter, waiting for Mrs. Owens to realize I'm up. Ruth Owens is more than my maid. She cooks, does my laundry, keeps my place clean, and, on occasion, provides me with wanted, or unwanted, advice. She's also jumpy and there's no way I'm tapping her on the shoulder. I clear my throat when she turns off the vacuum.

She whirls, slaps her hand to her chest, and says, "Mr. Pierce, you're going to scare me to death someday."

I can't hold back a chuckle. "I'm sorry. I decided it would be safer for me to wait over here until you discovered me. Something smells good."

"Blueberry muffins. I put a small pan of them in the oven. They'll be ready by the time you're dressed."

I cross the room to her and kiss the top of her head. "I don't know what I've done to deserve you."

She waves off my affection. "I wonder the same thing. Go, you slept in this morning." She shoos me out of the kitchen. "You're the only person I cook breakfast for this late. When are you going to live a normal life?"

"Why would I when I have you to take care of me?" I say over my shoulder as I head for the bathroom.

"I'm sixty-five years old. I'm not going to work forever. Who will keep food in your refrigerator when I'm gone?"

"Why are you here anyway? Today's a holiday." I'm dressed in dark jeans, a T-shirt, and white tennis shoes. When I make it back to the kitchen, scrambled eggs and two giant blueberry muffins are waiting for me on the counter. Mrs. Owens is gone, and a note is next to my plate. "Made a list of groceries and am going to the store."

"Go home," I tell her. Mrs. Owens doesn't bother to acknowledge my instructions.

My cell rings, and it's Nick Bianco, my friend, partner, and manager of our club, Gloss. "Morning."

"Are you coming to the office today?"

"Yeah. What's up?" Nick Bianco and Justin Locke, better known as Slider, have offices next door to my brokerage firm. It makes working together in the nightclub business convenient while keeping the two separate.

"Silder says he has good news."

"Great. I need you to cover for me tonight."

"No problem. Beth can run Gloss. You got a charity function?"

"No. I'm taking a date to dinner." I wait for the reaction I know is coming.

"A what?" Nick laughs in my ear. "Who are you? Better yet, who is she?"

"Just a woman I met at Gloss last night."

"Just? Don't try that shit on me. She must have a golden pussy for you to ask her out on a date."

"I can't answer that question yet. She's a gorgeous brunette with eyes the color of the sky on a summer day, not to mention she has a great body."

Nick sounds as if he gags. "That's almost sickening coming from your mouth. Must be one helluva woman."

"Maybe. I sense something about her. There's a fire there I'm going to explore."

"Bring her to Club Silken tonight. If she's got you horny, I definitely want a look at her."

"Something about her says she's ready for a change."

"I need to meet the woman who's piqued your interest."

I end the call wondering why it pisses me off Nick wants to get a look at Morgan. I fish my keys out of the bowl where I'd dropped them when I got home, ride the elevator down to the garage and make the drive to work. I drop my car off with the valet and walk up the ten flights to my suite of offices. Taking time to hit the gym gets harder every day. I need to stop putting it off and have a few pieces of equipment installed in one of the extra rooms in my apartment.

I'd established a successful brokerage business before Nick and Slider approached me with the idea of partnering to open three nightclubs. It has taken almost two years to get them up and running, but I've never regretted the partnership.

I step through the door into the hallway, walk to my suite of offices, and open the door into the waiting room. Walking past the receptionist's desk, I see my staff didn't forget today's a holiday. I find my assistant at my door, holding my coffee mug in her hand.

"Good afternoon, Mrs. Hayden. Why are you here?"

"I had a few things to catch up on. I'm leaving in a few minutes."

"Good." I take a sip of hot coffee. "You and the valet must have each other on speed dial."

"Whatever do you mean?"

"I get it. You have this sixth sense and know exactly when I will walk through the door."

"Of course." She gives me an innocent look. "I left three overtime vouchers on your desk for your initials, and for heaven's sake, go through those messages. People keep asking me the same questions over and over again."

"I'm on it." I take the cup of coffee from her, lean down, and kiss her cheek. "I love you too."

"That's sexual harassment," she quips.

"You like it," I fire back.

"Didn't say I didn't." As I walk into my office, she adds, "Check your email too."

Caroline Hayden is a fantastic woman. She's been with me since I started the business in a strip mall across town. She was in her early fifties then, so I'd put her at sixty-ish now. Always dressed to perfection, her sandy blonde hair doesn't have a trace of grey in it, and she has the posture of a model. Her sense of humor and loyalty are why she'll have a job here for as long as she wants.

I sit in my desk chair, log onto my computer, and dig into the stack of messages. Most are requests or invitations, and I write no thanks on the back of those. I only attend a few events to keep in the good graces with the local government, and I support a couple of charities I particularly like. I'm almost finished when Nick strolls into my office and goes straight to the minibar behind my desk.

"Slider's on his way." Nick pours three glasses of whiskey, hands me one, carries two, and takes a seat across from me.

"Do I need a drink?" I ask, trying to read his expression.

"You do for this toast."

Slider walks in with a big grin on his face. He takes one of the drinks and wastes no time with his news. "The receipts from last night at Gallants broke the grand opening record. We registered a higher headcount, and they were spending money."

"Congratulations. You've caught up with Gloss." I can't help but join Slider's excitement. He's three years younger than Nick and me and full of shit. Slider has a natural charisma that draws people to him. He likes people and it shows. Women fall all over themselves at his southern accent. "You were right about adding the band to bring in bigger profits."

Nick and I raise our glasses and Slider joins us. Afterward, we rehash last night's events at each club. Slider stands. "I've got paperwork to do."

"Did Zack tell you he has a date tonight?"

"No shit?" Slider plops back down into his chair

"I'm covering Silken for him tonight."

Slider's surprised expression is almost enough to make me laugh. "Zack, you have to stop by Gallants tonight. I need to check this chick out."

"What's with you two?" I turn my gaze on Nick.

Slider grins from ear to ear and leans forward, placing his elbows on his knees. "Come on, I need details, explicit details."

"Fuck you," I growl. "Find your own pussy." Immediately, I have a flash of guilt for talking about Morgan like that. Guilt isn't an emotion I'm familiar with, and I don't like it.

Slider and Nick exchange a silent look before Slider leans over and says, "This is gonna be good. I want all the details, Nick."

Both men leave my office and I can tell by their whispered conversation they're speculating about my mystery woman. I sort through a few messages but Morgan keeps popping into my thoughts. I call her to solidify our date.

"Hello."

"Morgan, it's Zack. I'm just confirming dinner tonight. Reservations are for seven-thirty." Who knows where we'll go from there, but I won't push her.

"I'm looking forward to it." I swear I can feel her smile over the phone. "I'm glad you called. Can you give me a hint as to where we're going? If we go to McDonald's, which is okay, I don't want to be overdressed." She sounds apprehensive, and I laugh, trying to ease her mind.

"Maybe I'll take you to McDonald's after I know you better. Tonight, we're having dinner at Chez Joey."

She laughs, and the sound makes me happy, another emotion I'm not all that familiar with. "Wow." That one word is all she says.

"The last thing you should worry about is how you'll look. You can wear a plastic grocery bag and still be stunning."

"Thank you. I'll try to live up to your compliment."

"I'll pick you up at seven, but only if I have your address."

"That would be helpful." I hear the smile in her voice. "I'll text it to you right now."

"Thanks." I end the conversation just as Nick and Slider walk past my office and wave goodbye. As always, Nick returns to my office and has one last thing to say on his way out. "You sure you don't want to tell me about this woman?" I've never known him to stick with one partner for over a few weeks.

"I'm sure. When did you turn into a nosey old woman?"

"You are so fucked. I've never seen your face light up over a woman since—" Nick stopped midsentence. "Sorry."

"Don't apologize. I'm happy she's married and someone else's problem. Get out of here. I'm right behind you."

Nick pauses in the doorway. His right eyebrow lifts. "I hope to see you and your new friend tonight."

"Go." I wave him off. Morgan has done a lot more than pique my interest. In those few minutes talking with her at the bar, a need started inside me I can only put out by sinking my dick deep inside her.

Chapter 2

Morgan

I changed dresses four times before deciding I couldn't go wrong with basic black. The front is modest with its high-neck, but the back is cut extremely low. Every time I walk past my full-length mirror I almost change again. But my makeup is just right and I've left my hair down, hanging well past my shoulders. Besides, I'm running out of time. My gut tells me Zackary Pierce isn't late for anything. I slip on a pair of red, open-toe, strappy heels that match the color of my toenails and fasten a long gold chain around my neck.

I sent Chels and Kayla to their apartments earlier, even though they'd begged to stay and check out Zack.

At precisely seven o'clock, I hear a knock on my door. I take a deep breath, wipe my sweaty palms on a hand towel, and go open the door.

Seeing Zack removes every word from my vocabulary. He's just fucking gorgeous, and I can't figure out why he wants me. His black suit fits his body perfectly, molding to hug his broad shoulders and narrow waist. It has to be tailor-made. His jacket is unbuttoned, revealing a crisp, white shirt with the collar open. I can't stop myself from pausing my gaze at the smattering of dark hair just above the buttons. Catching me checking him out, he smiles, and his dimple makes my blood warm. I clear my throat and manage to speak.

"Come in."

Zack smiles as he walks across my threshold. He lowers his head and places a soft kiss on my lips. I return his kiss, and the moment shifts from a sweet hello to a fuck-me-now version, with our tongues tasting the inside of each other's mouths. We are both panting hard when he steps back and says, "You take my breath away."

"Ditto," I lamely mumble, unable to compose a sentence. Around Zack, I lose all my inhibitions. He makes me feel free to express my sexuality and what I want, need, like, or dislike. Yet, I'm almost tongue-tied after that kiss.

His eyebrows lift. "Are you okay?"

"I am." I grab my knockoff Louis Vuitton clutch, lead him outside, and lock my door.

Zack takes my hand and escorts me down the stairs. I hear a loud whistle but ignore it. It happens again when we reach the visitor's parking lot.

"You have admirers," Zack says with a chuckle.

"Not me." I roll my eyes. "My friends Chelsea and Kayla are dying to get a look at you."

"Oh? What did you tell them about me?" His dark eyes twinkle with a hint of humor.

"I might have told them you're gorgeous and must be blind when you could be out with some beautiful model." I'm not sure how they'd react if they knew a visit to a members-only club might be on my agenda tonight. For some reason, I'm not ready to share that information.

He catches my chin, lifting it. "Don't doubt yourself. Ever. You are stunning, sexy, and mine." He turns around and bows to my friends. They both give us two thumbs up and grin as if they've never seen a living god before.

Zack escorts me to his sleek, red Porsche and whisks me away to one of the fanciest restaurants in Chicago. We leave his car with the valet and walk inside. Zack's hand is warm on my lower back. "Oh, baby," he whispers, softly running his fingers up and down my bare spine. "I love this dress."

"Thank you. It took me forever to decide what to wear."

"You have excellent taste in clothes." His voice is husky as we follow the hostess to a table in a far corner.

Chez Joey's décor is a subtle nod to New Orleans with its colorful Mardi Gras masks strategically placed on the walls, soft lighting, and jazz playing in the background. Zack selects our wine and tells the waiter to give us a few minutes to relax before we order.

We fall into easy conversation, discussing work, vacations, and ambitions. That changes when he asks about my family. I don't talk a lot about my youth, but he seems sincerely interested.

"I was ten when my parents died. They were on their way to celebrate my dad's promotion when a garbage truck ran a red light and slammed into their car."

Zack's eyes reflected my sadness. "That had to be tough. Losing a parent is hard, but you were so young. Then your Nana took you to raise?"

"Yes. She became my mom, dad, and best friend."

Zack extends his open hand across the table, and I place mine in his. His grip is warm and strong. "That's why your pink slippers are so important to you. Your grandmother gave you the love and guidance you needed."

"She did, and with the energy of a young woman. There wasn't a school function she missed." I blink away tears forming, but one escapes to trickle down my cheek. It happens every time I talk about her. "I lost her last year."

"Then I feel bad for teasing you about your slippers."

"Don't. I shouldn't be so sensitive." Talking about myself makes me feel vulnerable, so I changed the subject. "Tell me about your family."

"Family?" Zack scoffs and then tosses back the remainder of the wine in his glass. "I have a mother, father, and a younger brother. My parents divorced while I was in college, and both of them have remarried. My mom and her husband live in Provence, France. I haven't seen her since the separation. My brother, Simon, is thirty-one and following in the footsteps of our dear old dad." Zack's tone is harsh when he speaks of his family.

"Do you see your father often?"

"Not if I can help it. More than ten minutes in a room with him, and we're both pissed off. I quit trying to please him a long time ago."

Our waiter appears, and the family discussion is dropped, leaving me with many questions. Zack and I both order shrimp creole and coffee. Service is fast and we quickly fall into an easy silence while eating.

When the waiter stops by to clear our table, Zack orders Baileys for both of us. He leans back in his chair and studies me for a minute.

"You're staring." I sigh, relieved I hadn't spilled food on my dress.

"So is every man in the restaurant."

"Please." I smile, appreciating the compliment.

"You honestly don't know how beautiful you are?"

"Have you considered they might be staring at you?"

"No." His laugh rolls up from deep in his chest. I want to hear it again. "If that's true, they're wasting their time."

His gaze deepens, and I feel he can see inside me. "What's on your mind?"

"I'm trying to decide what to do next."

"We're not going to your club?" Heat rushes from my neck to my cheeks. Is our date going to end so quickly?

"I'm not sure about taking you to Silken tonight."

"Why? Do I come across as scared?"

"Not scared, but maybe a little naïve. I won't push you into going."

"I'm perfectly capable of saying stop."

One corner of Zack's mouth lifts upward. "You researched BDSM today, didn't you?"

He's grinning at me, watching as my face gets hotter. "Yes, and there are a few things I find outrageous."

"Tell me."

"I'm not the type to allow anybody to whip me with a cat o' nine tails and I'm not going to lick anybody's shoes."

His lips spread even wider, flashing straight, white teeth and that sexy dimple. "I don't use whips or paddles and I can shine my own shoes. However, I'm not beyond spanking my sub's ass if she needs it."

My heart plummeted. "You have a sub?"

"No, I don't. Haven't for a long time."

"Is it rude of me to ask what happened?"

"No. It's a fair question. My brokerage firm keeps me busy as hell, and the past two years getting three clubs open and profitable has taken up my every free minute. My last sub needed a dom who could spend more time and attention on her, so I helped her find the perfect person. They're very happy."

"Really? She was okay with you finding her another sex partner?"

"Yes. She'd attended the club with a friend and came back with an interest in being trained as a sub. I was available and offered my time. After a few months, we agreed she was ready for more. It wasn't as if we'd entered into the relationship with the understanding it would be permanent."

"I think not getting attached would be difficult."

"It depends on what the expectations are going in. There are different levels of dom/sub relationships. Some couples are committed to following the lifestyle in every facet of their lives. Not all do though. In fact, some members are married. They join to spice up their sex lives. Some men and women enjoy being restrained and punished. We offer private and open rooms because some of our members like having an audience. I'll show you if you're sure you're interested."

"Can I just observe?" A cross between curiosity and excitement floods my senses.

"Absolutely. Not everyone partners up every time they come to the club. If a man or woman comes alone, he or she might be invited to participate. Regardless of who you are, no means no. Nothing takes place at my club without each party's explicit agreement."

My mind is racing. I'm freaking out at how drawn I am to Zack, and, yet, I don't know if I'm ready for another disappointment. He's watching my face as if reading every thought.

"If you need time to think it over, take it. I'm not going anywhere." His dark eyes reflect a sincerity that weakens my reserve.

I open my mouth but quickly close it.

"Talk to me." Zack leans closer, and the heat from his body comforts me.

"I want to see this through."

"Me too." His face lights up. "I'll do my best to earn your trust and always put your pleasure and safety first. It's the trust that makes any successful dom/sub relationship work. You can stop any action with one word."

"I'd like to go to Silken with you," I say bravely. One side of his mouth quirks up in a smile, making me swallow hard.

"There's nowhere else I'd rather take you." There's a "but" in there somewhere so I hold my breath and wait. "I'm very attracted to you, Morgan. The last thing I want is to frighten you away."

"I don't scare easily, and I want to see where this thing between us goes."

Zack's eyebrow arches. "Are you always so open to experiencing new things?"

I consider my answer for a few seconds. "Not usually. I've never been in a situation where I could explore different sexual wants and needs. No one's ever asked me what I like or dislike. Maybe I can discover those things with you. The idea intrigues me."

"Brave girl. I'll not only ask you questions, but I'll also remember your responses." Zack drops cash on the table, stands, and pulls back my chair. He shifts my hair over one shoulder and brushes the spot under my earlobe with his lips. "Let's go," he whispers.

Minutes after the valet brings the car around, Zack and I are on the freeway cruising south. Twenty minutes later he takes an exit and after a few turns, we're on an unmarked road. With no lights except the car's headlights, we drive through the darkness. The farther we go, the faster my heart beats. I lean forward and peer out the windshield searching for the club.

"They're not going to find my mutilated dead body in a field of hay, are they?"

"No." Zack's laugh is strong and fills his sports car with a deep, rich sound. "I meant it when I said you can trust me." He puts his hand on my bare knee and fire rolls up my leg.

"Since we've established you're not a serial killer, may I ask a personal question?"

"Let me see if I can answer without you asking." His touch on my thigh is distracting, and I'm hoping his hand keeps moving upward. He glances over at me. "No, I'm not married, nor do I have any children. I am divorced. It ended badly. How about you?"

"Nice way to turn the conversation back on me."

"I thought so." Zack flashes his dimple and my pussy clenches. "Your turn."

"Never married and no children. A couple of boyfriends but nothing stuck."

"What else do we need to share?"

"Nothing comes to mind, but I'm sure I'll think of something later." This is the truth because I want to know more about him as a person. "I tried to research Club Silken today but couldn't find one mention of it."

"That's exactly as planned. We do zero advertising. It's an elite club and membership comes at a high price and with a recommendation from a trusted member. Once a comprehensive background check is completed on the applicant, and he or she reads and signs the documents required they're accepted. Likewise, we insist on secrecy. Only first names are used inside the club, and if a member prefers anonymity, we're happy to provide a mask."

"Anonymous sex. Interesting." I squirm in my seat.

"If you'd be more comfortable, I'll get you a mask. We offer our members and guests safety, privacy, and respect to ensure their sexual predilections are protected." Zack puts both hands on the wheel and my body immediately goes into withdrawal. "Sorry. I sound like a salesman."

I finally see lights in the distance and with a couple more turns, we stop in front of a sprawling house that could have been used in an old western movie. There are no signs welcoming customers inside. The only indication the place is anything other than a large family residence is the number of cars in a side parking lot.

Zack drives under a portico, stops, and waves off the valet. He gets out and walks around to my side of the car. He opens my door, takes my hand, and helps me out of the car.

"Do I look all right for this crowd?"

"You're perfect." He runs his thumb across my lower lip and sandwiches me between his hard body and the car, crushing his lips against mine. Our tongues delve inside each other's mouths. I swear I could live on his taste while his scent reminds me of an ocean breeze and sunshine. Zack breaks our kiss and cups my cheeks in his hands. "You're going to be the death of me."

"I certainly hope not." What the hell is going on inside my head? A strange woman has taken possession of my mind. Whoever she is, I like her. A lot.

Zack leads me up the steps to the house and a mountain of a man opens the door. He steps aside so we can enter.

"Good evening."

"Gabriel," Zack says. "Is everything running smoothly tonight?"

"As always."

"Morgan this is Gabriel. No one gets past him unless they're a member or escorted by one. You'll see him on the floor from time to time making sure all policies of the club are followed."

"Nice to meet you, ma'am." He closes the exterior door behind us and moves to stand behind a desk next to a set of double doors. "Anybody messes with you, just ask one of our monitors for assistance. They're easy to spot in their red silk vests."

"Thank you, I'll do that." If either of them caught the nervous twinge in my voice, they don't react.

Gabriel hands me a clipboard. "Guests must fill out a consent and nondisclosure form before they enter."

I look up at Zack and he nods. "Always read before you sign anything."

"No problem." I read over the rules and the promise to reveal nothing about the club or what happens inside. I sign and pass the clipboard back to Gabriel. He wraps a white, silk ribbon around my right bicep. I shiver with the realization that he's just marked me as Zack's. Tonight, the members will know I belong to him. *Can I live up to what that means?*

Zack answers my unasked question. "Our members will welcome you, but they won't invite you to participate in anything." Zack opens the interior door and slow, sexy music drifts out to meet us. "Would you feel more comfortable wearing a mask?"

"No. I don't think I know anybody who has enough money to belong to this club."

"Enjoy." Gabriel closes the doors behind us, and I'm standing in a new world.

"Can you tell I'm nervous?" I'm trying to relax but haven't yet. Zack's hand drops to the bare skin on my back.

"Remember, nothing happens unless you ask me for it. Would you like a tour?"

"Yes, if it comes with explanations."

"That's my brave girl." He places a soft kiss on my forehead.

"We'll see." My curiosity is high and my body is trembling as if all my appendages have just received an electric shock.

"Let's get a drink. I'll introduce you to Nick first. He's the manager of Gloss but he's covering for me here tonight."

The bar is white, polished marble with grey swirls running through it. Dark grey, padded leather stools run the length of the bar, but they're mostly empty. I'm about to ask where everybody is when a male walks out from behind the bar. Wearing black slacks that hug his hips and a black, long-sleeve shirt with the top buttons left open, he runs his hand through his hair and walks toward me. He doesn't glance at Zack, instead, he zeroes in on me with open arms.

"I don't think so." Zack extends his arm in front of me with a chuckle. "Morgan, this is Nick. Never be alone with him."

I look up at Zack. "Why?"

"I'll have to kill him."

"Welcome to Club Silken." Nick's smile gets wider as his gaze travels the length of my body and back up to my face. "Zack wasn't lying when he said you're a knockout. Don't take that white ribbon off or we'll have a stampede."

"Thank you. I think." Heat rises to my face at Nick's compliment. This feeling of belonging to someone is new to me, and I'm surprised at how much I like it. Even the low growl coming from Zack excites me. He sounds jealous and protective.

"How about making yourself useful and getting us something to drink." Zack and I stop at the first two stools. He takes my hand and helps me get seated. "We serve alcohol to members at no charge, but there's a two drink maximum."

"I read that in the rules and I agree keeping the alcohol intake under control is a great idea."

"We also have soft drinks, orange juice, or water. Your choice," Nick says while grinning at Zack.

"Water, please." Nick turns and says something to the bartender and a minute later, I have a glass of ice and a bottle of Soma, which just happens to be one of the most expensive waters in the world. This stuff sells for thirty bucks a bottle.

"Zack, you want something?"

"Maybe later." He and Nick talk for a minute so I turn on my stool and take a closer look at my surroundings.

The dance floor is crowded with couples who are barely swaying to the music. My heart beats faster as I watch a man slide the straps off his partner's shoulders, leans down and licks her bare nipple right there in front of all those people. She bows her back lifting higher and giving the man better access to her breasts. Her eyes cast downward watching him as he sucks her into his mouth. My breasts tighten at the erotic scene, and, for a minute, I can't pull my gaze away.

Plush leather couches with side tables fill one area close to the bar. Normally I wouldn't be shocked seeing two men leaning back casually talking with each other. It's the naked women kneeling beside each one of them that keeps me from looking away. Hands clasped behind their backs, heads tilted downward, their hair is being stroked like they're pet Collies.

A loud crack accompanied by a woman's cry jerks my attention away from the couples to somewhere farther back in the club. My heart races faster and nerves I never knew existed prickle throughout my body.

I pull my gaze away and turn to find Zack leaning against the counter, legs crossed at the ankles, watching me. His eyes are dark with a predatory passion. He leans down and whispers, "Ready for your tour?"

Hoping my legs won't fail me, I take one long swallow of my expensive water and nod. "Let's do this."

"You may see things that unnerve you, shock you, and, hopefully, excite you. Not only will I be with you, remember the men wearing red vests monitor everything that goes on throughout the building to ensure members' safety." Zack pulls my hand to his mouth and kisses my palm. As he leads me away, I clutch his hand tightly, ready to see the rest of his club.

"Do the monitors have to intervene a lot?"

"Actually, no. Members are always sober and consenting. We enforce the rules, so if someone is too tipsy, their partner must decline the evening's activities. Seldom does anyone become overzealous. I can't say it's never happened, but swift action is taken, and the offending person loses their membership."

I hear that cry again. "That's the second time I've heard a woman cry out."

"Let's take a look." Zack guides me to an area where sections are divided by ropes. "This is where open scenes take place. Members can merely watch or, if one is not in use, they can use it for their own scene." He squeezes my hand and leads me down the aisle where a small crowd has gathered.

I see a naked woman bound by ropes to some sort of wooden device. Dozens of emotions rush my brain. I'm still trying to sort them out when Zack pulls me in front of him.

"It's called a Saint Andrew's Cross," he whispers.

"Please. Please," the woman whimpers as tears streak down her cheeks. The man hangs up his cane and gently rubs her fiery red ass. "Please, Sir. I need to come," she pleads.

"Questions?" Zack stands behind me with his hands on my waist. His warm breath on my neck sends a shiver throughout my body.

"She's not asking him to stop. She's begging for permission to come?"

"Yes. These two have been a couple since before this club opened. Both know exactly what to expect when they come through the door. It's their favorite scene, and they enjoy being watched."

"But she's crying."

"Pain and pleasure are the same things to some people. In her case, the pain is sweet and releases endorphins that enhance her orgasm."

The man's hand disappears between the woman's legs. "Come for me, now," he commands.

The woman's head falls back and a look of pure ecstasy fills her face as her body jerks. Her moans are loud and erotic as her orgasm overtakes her. By the time the man brings his wet fingers to his mouth and licks them clean, I'm aware of the moisture soaking my panties. When her restraints are removed, the crowd thins and people move away. The man gently wraps her in a blanket, lifts her in his arms, and carries her out of sight.

I lean back against Zack, almost melting his arms. "Where's he taking her?"

"To a quiet area where he'll hold her until she regains her strength."

"I'm exhausted from watching. I'm sure she needs quiet after that."

Zack turns me and places his forehead to mine. "You're a passionate woman."

"You think?" I try teasing.

"If I slide my hand under your dress will I discover your pussy is soaking wet?"

His question surprises me and my mouth dries up. "Yes."

"We'd better move on." Zack's breathing hard, telling me he's as turned on as I am.

We pause at a scene where a man is sprawled in a red velvet chair watching another man suck his dick deep into his throat. I feel Zack's eye's on me, not the men. No doubt, he's measuring my reaction. The rapid rise and fall of my chest must show him how much this turns me on.

"We'll take a right at the end of this aisle. I want to show you a few of the theme rooms."

Zack pauses to say hello to a few members as we head toward the back of the club. It doesn't escape me that most of the women keep their heads and gazes lowered. The females who are free to look around glare daggers at me as we pass by. I smile with pride because Zack doesn't seem to notice them.

"About half of the building is made up of private rooms with doors that lock. They're down the back wall and are reserved in advance. The staff prepares the scene requested with everything the member will need to act out their fantasy. Let me show you." He escorts me inside one. "An open door is an invitation to join in the activities. A red light comes on over the door when the lock is engaged. The occupants decide if they want privacy or will allow outside viewing. The rooms on the other side of the club have theater-style seating and curtains."

The room we're in is decorated like a Regency ballroom from the 1800s. A crystal chandelier, complete with candles, hangs from the ceiling and tapestries cover the walls. Male and female period costumes are on display in an open closet in the corner. My gaze is drawn to what I assume will be used for punishment. "Stocks?"

Zack shrugs. "That was harder to find than I expected. It had to be specially made."

I open a cabinet and step back, laughing. "There are enough condoms, vibrators, and toys in here to last a very long time." I lift out a box of condoms. "It's not exactly authentic since these didn't exist in the early 1800s. Well, not until the French letter was invented."

"We humans have made a little progress." His smile tells me he's enjoying himself. "Since we're on the subject of condoms, I'll set up an appointment to have both of us tested."

"I've been taking the pill for a long time."

"The test is to assure both of us are healthy and are without a communicable disease. It's a house rule and one of mine."

I'm stunned into silence. He spit that out as if this is an everyday conversation.

"Once we're comfortable with the results, I won't use protection. I prefer the intimacy of skin on skin."

My system is on complete overload. But he's making plans for more than tonight and I can't hold back my smile. "Uh, okay."

"I've shocked you?"

"No. Yes." I'm lost in his knowing smile. "A little, but I understand."

"It's for both our safety." He moves me around the room. "What else do you see?"

I concentrate on the question and form my answer. "Snow-white towels, washcloths, and a blanket." I open a drawer and find a riding crop, paddle, leather cuffs, and several bottles of water. "I can imagine keeping hydrated would be important." I'm joking, but Zack nods.

"Let's look in on a room in use." He takes my hand and leads me past a couple of closed doors. "There's an individual hallway behind each one that allows viewers if the participants wish. This particular couple opens the two-way mirror because it enhances their enjoyment. Ready?"

"I think so."

"That's my brave girl." He leads me behind one of the rooms and stops.

I suck in a breath and blink a couple of times. I wouldn't have described myself as a voyeur but I can't look away from the beautiful expression on the woman's face. She's lying on a table with her feet in stirrups. A man wearing a white medical coat pulls her body so her butt is almost hanging off the edge. I clench my thighs when he spreads her pussy lips open, leans down, and laps at her with his tongue like he's starving and she's an all you can eat buffet. I don't know how long we've watched when a second man steps in. His hands cup her breasts and he sucks a nipple into his mouth.

"She can stop this anytime but she never does. They're a married couple who schedules a threesome every month or two. Sometimes with a man and sometimes a woman."

I can't speak. The scene is so erotic my knees are weak.

Zack steps behind me. His erection throbs against my back, and I push my ass closer to him. The two men intensify their actions. One enters her while the other climbs on top of the table holding his cock to her lips. Her tongue slides out and across the tip. She licks the precum off his tip before opening wide and allowing him to sink deep into her throat. Her hands grasp his hips as he fucks her mouth.

"Oh, my God." I turn my head, searching for Zack's lips.

His kiss is hard, and his tongue slashes into my mouth. His hands slide up my sides, stopping near my breasts. I am so out of control with need, I turn into his touch.

"Remember, nothing happens without your permission." He slides my hair over one shoulder. His breath caresses that spot right under my earlobe. "I want to touch you but I need to hear you say yes or no."

"Yes," I whisper without hesitation.

He cups my left breast and thumbs my rigid nipple while he's slowly lifting my skirt. I moan when my wet panties are moved to the side and his hand cups my saturated pussy. Without thinking, I spread my legs open for him and he dips a finger inside me.

"Zack," I groan when he adds a second finger, slowly pumping in and out while we watch the men on the other side of the glass continue making love to the woman. Her back is bowed and her eyes are wide open.

"Come for me." Zack's thumb grinds against my clit, and I explode, pumping against his hand. Waves of pleasure take control of my mind and body as my orgasm surges through me again and again. I clamp my legs together, holding his fingers inside me until the tremors subside. My legs turn to rubber, but Zack slides one arm around my waist holding me steady and turns me to face him.

He puts his fingers into his mouth and sucks them clean, just as the man did in the first scene we watched. These new experiences have me on overload and my juices start trickling out again. "Zack," I moan.

"I knew you'd taste good. I can't wait to spread your pussy open and get a first-hand taste." He straightens my dress, lifts me in his arms, and I snuggle into his neck. He carries me across the club as if I'm the most precious thing he's ever held in his arms.

We sit in a quiet corner and I lift my head to look up into his eyes. "That was spectacular." Reality hits and I'm shocked at my behavior. "Oh, my God, I can't believe I did that in public."

"Did what? Allowed yourself to be sexually pleasured in a hallway? With me, you never have to feel embarrassed by your sexuality." His mouth finds mine and he slides his tongue inside. I taste myself as the kiss slowly builds until I'm squirming on his lap. He pulls back and wipes a strand of hair from my face. "I want you to be open and free with me."

"Am I surprised at myself? Yes. Would I do it again? Hell, yes." I burrow my face deeper into his neck.

Zack shifts me so he can look into my eyes. "I'm glad you want more because I love how responsive you are."

"I want more. A lot more."

His hips shift under me. "Fuck. I'm still hard and holding you in my lap isn't helping."

"Want me to do something about that?"

His lips brush my forehead. "Tempting, but tonight is about you, not me."

That he denied himself impresses me. "I think I'd like more of that water I left behind."

"Want me to carry you?"

I kiss him this time. God, I love his lips and mouth. "No, thanks. If my knees get weak, I'll lean on you."

We take a different path to the bar, passing more open scene rooms. I see a woman spanking a man with a wooden paddle and he seems to be enjoying himself. In the next one, a naked woman is kneeling between two men. Fully dressed with their pants unzipped, their legs are spread wide and each is holding his cock out while she moves back and forth between them. She pulls off the guy closest to us and he grabs her hair.

"Don't stop. I'm going to come." The man groans, lifting his hips toward her.

"Wait for me. I want it all." She takes him deep into her mouth until his pubic hair brushes her face. Her throat works as she swallows and swallows.

I'm mesmerized and turn my face to Zack. He's looking at me with that passionate dark glare of his. It's exactly the way I'm feeling about him. "Oh. My. God. Can you say sensory overload?"

He clears his throat. "But do any of the scenes we've watched interest you?"

"It's a lot to take in at one time, but so far, everything here interests me."

"I like the sound of that."

"Everything except the cane."

"Duly noted." Zack nods and his dark hair tumbles onto his forehead. I step closer and brush it into place with my fingers.

We sit on the same stools we used when we first arrived and both drink water. Zack's friend Nick is on one of the couches talking with a man and woman. He waves and joins us. Can he tell I just had a major orgasm? Do I care?

"What do you think of the club?" Nick asks.

I take a drink of water and think about how to answer his question. "It's amazing. I understand the need for a place like this. It's a safe haven where you can be comfortable in your own skin and where nobody judges you." I glance at Zack, and he shows me his approval with a wide smile.

"Well said, Morgan."

"I heard you were at Gloss the night Zack closed for me," Nick says. "What did you think about my club?"

"I really like it. The dance floor is awesome, the people are friendly, but I lost my billfold. If I hadn't, I wouldn't have met Zack."

"I'm hungry again." Zack's still beaming at me with that panty-melting smile. "Let's go find somewhere that serves dessert."

"You're on." I stand to shake hands with Nick and find myself scooped into a hug.

"Enough," Zack growls.

"When you get tired of this guy come and see me."

"That day will never come." Zack takes my hand and we walk out through the double doors.

"I'll call for your car." Gabriel starts to tap something into his cell.

"Don't. We'll walk."

"Okay." Gabriel reaches across the desk for the silk white ribbon on my arm.

"May I keep it?" I hope Zack's going to ask me out again, but, regardless, I never want to forget this night. The way he took care of my need without concern for himself is permanently recorded in my brain.

Gabriel smiles and steps back from me. "The boss's lady gets anything she wants."

My heart jumps. The boss's lady sounds amazing. "Thank you."

"Good night." Zack slaps the big guy on his arm then takes my hand.

"Drive safely."

When the outside door closes, Zack stops on the top step. "Are you all right?"

"Good question." I lick my dry lips. "It was the education of a lifetime."

"Oh." He smoothes my hair back over my shoulders. "Tonight was the first grade. I'm going to enjoy taking you all the way to graduation."

Chapter 3

Zack

"What's your choice for dessert?" I drive away from Silken, aware my dick is screaming. We need to fuck and soon. The target, of course, is Morgan. I, on the other hand, don't want to steamroll her into anything too soon. She's already surprised me on so many levels.

"When you said dessert, were you talking about food or sex?" she asks in a soft voice.

I stop the car in the middle of the dark road, unhook my seatbelt, lean across, and kiss the hell out of her. "I'm good with either one as long as it gets me another date with you."

"I'd love to see you again."

"It's a plan." I buckle up and restart our trip back to Chicago. Morgan needs to talk about tonight and I need to know she's okay so far with my lifestyle. "What kind of ice cream do you like?"

"Is there a flavor not to like? If I have to choose, I'd say vanilla with chocolate syrup and whipped cream."

"Careful saying chocolate and whipped cream around me." I reach across and rest my hand on her bare thigh. "It put an image in my head of you in my bed while I lick you clean."

Morgan turns toward me. Her mouth is slightly gaping.

"Do I shock you by telling the truth?"

"No. Yes." She shifts in her seat and her dress rises higher up her legs. "That gave me a full-body shiver." Her words are barely above a whisper.

I tighten my grip on her thigh. "I know. I felt it."

"I thought I was going to self combust a couple of times tonight." Her voice is so soft I barely hear her.

"Morgan, will you come home with me?" I love her honesty and I straighten my arm reaching farther up her thigh until I'm brushing the edge of her panties. I hold my breath like a kid who hopes he's getting the Christmas present he's been begging for.

"Yes. I want you."

I hit the accelerator a little harder and head home. "Morgan, there are a few more things you need to know about me. As I explained, my life is too cluttered and I don't want a slave who awaits my every command. I like a woman with a brain, which means I'll support you and your career.

"When we're at my club or in the bedroom, I expect your complete submission. When I give you instructions, you'll not argue with me. I control your body and your orgasms. Your pleasure is my responsibility." I stop talking, giving her a few minutes to digest what I said. "I will push your limits, but I'll never go past your hard line unless you ask me to. That doesn't mean I won't test you, but you have the final say."

I can feel her gaze on the side of my face. Just as I think she's going to tell me to fuck off, she sighs. "I like the idea of you being responsible for my pleasure."

"Take off your panties. Then turn back toward me with your legs spread." Morgan doesn't hesitate. She wiggles out of her panties, drops them on the floor of my car, and follows my instructions to the letter.

I wish it was daylight so I could see her better. I force myself to keep my eyes on the road while my hand slides up her thigh until I reach warm, wet skin. A moan rolls from her, and she lifts her hips higher, allowing me to slide two fingers inside her. I stroke a couple of times before finding her clit with my thumb. Morgan scoots as close to me as her seatbelt will allow. She's so open and willing, but I can't reward her yet. "Does that feel good?"

She clenches around my fingers and groans. "Oh, yes."

"Do not come." I use a firm tone of voice to ensure she understands.

"But I'm so close." She's panting hard and right on the edge so I remove my fingers. "No. Don't stop."

"Do not tell me what to do." For the second time tonight, I lick her juices from my fingers. "We talked about this. Tell me who is in charge of your orgasms?"

"You are," she grumbles.

I almost laugh at her reply, but I don't. Instead, I use an icy tone. "Are you arguing with me?"

"Uh, was I?"

"Turn in your seat, straighten your dress, and then hand me your panties."

"Okay," she whispers.

I stuff her panties in my pocket. "You won't need these again tonight." I turn into my garage and quickly park. She's standing next to the car when I walk around to her. "Next time, wait for me to open your door."

"Okay." She licks her lips, and I want to fuck her right here against the car.

"I can't tell you how painfully hard my dick has been all night."

"I want you inside me." Her fingers grasp me through my slacks and I push her hand away.

"We'll get to that later. Tonight you will not come until I'm buried deep inside your pussy. Understood?"

Morgan's blue eyes lift and hold my gaze. "Yes. I want that too."

I push her back against the hood of my car and claim her mouth. The kiss is demanding and forceful with me thrusting my tongue in and out. I need to get her on my bed so I scoop her in my arms and carry her to the elevator.

Morgan tucks her face into my neck and licks from under my jaw down past the pounding vein in my neck. "Wherever we're going, please hurry."

The doors swish open, and I cross my living room, heading straight to the stairs. I don't stop until we're in my bedroom and at the foot of my bed. I set her feet on the floor and she stands there waiting. I slip my hands under her long hair and unsnap her dress. In seconds I have her naked. She's an exquisite sight in her red heels. I move away and stare at her stunning body. Her creamy breasts have perfect, rose-colored nipples that are just waiting for my mouth. My gaze follows her narrow waist and curvy hips down to her smooth pussy with a dark landing strip sitting above my prize. My mouth waters and my cock is leaking precum. "Fuck, Morgan. You're more beautiful than I imagined."

"Thank you." Her smile tells me she's delighted with my response to her body.

"Take off your shoes then move to the middle of the bed. Bend your knees and spread your legs wide. I need to see how wet you are for me."

Morgan toes off her heels then climbs on the bed and then crawls on her hands and knees to the middle, showing me her soft, round ass. When she shifts to her back and hesitates before spreading her legs, I can't pull my gaze away. I've had one long-term relationship and it turned to shit. But seeing how Morgan responds and wants to please me, I know in my gut, I'm not going to tire or be bored with her for a long time. Until then, I'm going to enjoy pushing every one of her boundaries.

****

Morgan

Zack's gaze sears my skin, torching my blood as moisture pools between my legs. His black shirt comes off and flies across the room. I suck in a breath, almost blurting out that he's beautiful. His bare chest and abdomen are defined with chiseled muscles. A dusting of black hair spreads across his pecs, tapering to a thin trail that makes its way over washboard abs, past the defined V at his hips, and disappears under the waistband of the slacks he's wearing. My gaze follows that path to the large bulge in his slacks. Oh, my God, he's huge.

Without taking his eyes off my pussy, he kneels in front of me. "Lift your hips." His voice has dropped an octave, and his brown eyes have darkened to almost black. He reaches above my head, grabs a pillow, and slides it under me.

When I settle on the cushion beneath me, he leans forward and runs his index finger back and forth through my wetness, teasing me like a cat with his paw on a mouse's tail.

"Fucking gorgeous."

My pussy is throbbing and swollen with lust. I'm afraid I'll blast off like a rocket if he touches my clit. I reach for him but he shakes his head.

"I didn't give you permission to touch me. Put your arms behind your head, fingers laced. Do not move them until I tell you too. Understand?"

I nod, but Zack's eyes narrow. "Yes, Sir," I quickly add.

"When we're in my bed, I need you to speak your responses."

"Yes, Sir," I say again with more sincerity.

Zack gets on the bed and moves up to where my feet are planted. His thumb and finger spread my outer lips. His gaze is intense as he looks at my most sensitive parts. "Morgan, this is the sexiest sight I've ever seen. I can't wait any longer to taste this pretty, pink pussy of yours." Closing my eyes, I melt when his tongue licks me from back to front in one long, slow stroke. He does it again, lapping up every drop of my wetness.

My hips lift off the pillow of their own accord and a low groan rolls from deep in my chest. Every nerve in my body fires heat signals straight to my clit, which is throbbing and begging for attention.

"I fucking knew you'd taste like peaches and cream."

"I do not."

Zack lifts his head and raises one eyebrow. "That's twice you've argued with me. Fair warning. Do it again and I'll spank your sweet ass." Zack nips the soft skin on my thigh. "Watch. Feel. Enjoy. Do not come."

He said watch and the only way for me to do that is to prop myself up on my elbows, which means moving my hands, which I do in time to see him lower his head between my thighs. He explores every inch of my pussy, licking and tasting before driving his tongue inside me; sending shock waves up my spine to my brain.

"God. That feels so good." I drop my head to the bed and stretch my arms back into position above my head. The last thing I want is for him to stop.

His tongue, wet with my juices, lashes my clit back and forth while I squirm. The heel of his hand moves to the top of my mound and his thumb and forefinger pull the hood away from my clit, baring it to the base.

"Your clit is hard and very needy." He sucks me into his hot mouth and flattens his tongue, pressing and releasing. The pleasure pushes me to the edge and has me writhing under him.

"Zack. Oh, God, please, I need to come." I think I said the words, but I'm gasping for air and moaning at the same time. My entire body shudders. Two fingers slide inside me, curve, and rub my G-spot. "Zack," I cry out, pleading.

"Since you've been such a brave girl tonight, you may come."

"Yes." I lift my hips higher and unashamedly fuck his face. My orgasm hits and my body jerks wildly as wave after wave of release sucks me under, pulling me into the deep. I wilt and float to the surface, panting like an overheated runner. "So good. So good."

Zack kisses his way up my body until he reaches my lips. His tongue slips into my open mouth. He tastes of me, and my body reacts with need. I nip his bottom lip, loving the low growl that comes from him.

"God, you are so responsive." Zack grabs a condom from the bedside table. "I need to be inside you."

"Yes, please," I whispered. "I want to feel you." I open my legs wide, waiting while he rips open the package and covers himself.

He pushes my legs even wider and settles himself at the apex of my thighs. Leaning in, he rubs his cock against my folds. I lock my legs around his waist, trying to push myself onto his erection.

Zack's still sliding back and forth through my wetness, nudging my clit with each stroke. He wraps his hand around his dick and coats the condom with my moisture to ease his entry. He slips just the head inside me and then stops.

"Please, Zack. Fuck me hard."

"Hold yourself open." His gaze follows the movement of my hands.

Almost out of my mind with need, I don't hesitate. "How's this?"

"Perfect. Now I can watch my cock sink inside you." His lips lift into a smile as he stares at me, spread open before him. "I will never get tired of this view."

If a rapid heartbeat can crack a rib, I'm on the verge of shattering a few. I lift my head to watch his cock drive into my core. He pushes deeper inside me, slowly moving forward and back, giving me the time to adjust to his girth. He's long and thick, so I lift my hips to give him better access to my body. "More."

His hands grip my hips, holding me still. "I decide when you get more. This is my pussy. Say it."

"Yes, Sir. This is your pussy." I gasp as he slams inside me and the head of his dick bottoms out. I spasm a couple of times as my body adjusts to his size. I moan and silently plead for more.

"What was it you wanted?"

"You inside me." He's not moving and I'm ready to scream.

"That's not what you asked for."

My brain scrambles. "You to fuck me hard."

"Yes." Zack pulls out until I can barely feel the tip of his dick inside me and then he slams home.

"Just like that." My body is blazing with need. I grasp his biceps and hang on tightly.

His hands slide under my ass and lift me so he can penetrate even deeper. He pummels me again and again. Sweat beads on his forehead, but he doesn't slow down. I hover on the edge, not wanting him to stop and, yet, trying to hold off my orgasm. Grinding his pelvis against me, he pinches one of my nipples.

"Come now," he commands.

I detonate. Lights explode behind my eyes, shattering stars into space in wild, violent bursts. Zack continues to pump in and out as my inner walls clench and pull him deeper into my greedy need to take everything he has to give.

"Fuck." Zack groans a primal sound as he pulses inside me, coming so hard I feel it through the condom. The sensation prolongs my climax.

He relaxes his forearms and lays flat against me. Our sweat mingles and our bodies become one for a few minutes. I actually may have purred. Zack lifts back up on his elbows, taking some of his weight off me. A smile lights his face.

"That was fucking fantastic."

"Yes, it was."

He brushes the hair off my face, kissing as he moves down to my neck. His touch is glorious. He rolls us onto our sides, facing each other, with his semi-erect dick still inside me. Neither of us moves, instead, he rests his forehead against mine.

When he pulls out, I protest. "Don't go."

"Hang on." He laughs. "I'll be right back." He gets up, removes the condom, ties it off, and carries it into the bathroom. I hear the water running and soon he returns with a washcloth. He spreads my legs and washes me with the warm rag. My heart pinches and I turn my head away.

"Did I hurt you?" His soulful eyes search my face.

"No. Not at all." My heart melts at his concern.

"I must have."

He isn't going to let this go so I take a deep breath. "Truth?"

"Truth."

"You surprised me. Nobody has ever treated me with such tenderness and caring." I lean my face into his hand. His thumb caresses my cheek.

"That changes tonight." Zack winds a lock of my hair around his finger. His eyebrows relax and his dark eyes finally shine. "Since I didn't hurt you . . ." He's hard again, and his erection pushes against my thigh. He rolls over onto his back, lifts his cock with his hand and says, "Take me in your mouth."

"With pleasure." I slide down the bed and lick the precum off the tip of his dick. "I'll never be too tired, too busy, or too sore for you." His length and girth will take some adjusting on my part. I pause, swirl my tongue around him, lubricating his silky skin. I relax my jaw, sliding him to the back of my throat, I pump up and down, taking him as deep as I can.

"Fuck," he moans, lifting his hips and pulling my hair away from my face. His groan comes from deep in his chest. I pull back to the tip and give his slit an open mouth kiss. The sounds he makes encourages me so I slide my lips to the base of his cock and kiss until I've touched every inch of him. Pausing to pay attention to the little nubbin of flesh underneath the crown has Zack is muttering words I don't understand.

Cupping his balls in my hand, I gently massage them while I take him deeply again and again until his precum and my saliva run down my chin.

I lift my gaze to his face.

"You're so fucking hot with your lips wrapped around my cock." His tug on my hair tightens and his eyes lock with mine. I want to taste everything he gives me. I want to see his face when he comes.

"I'm coming. Fuck." His body stiffens for a split second before he starts fucking my mouth in earnest.

I concentrate on pulling him deep into the back of my throat with each stroke. His dick swells and hot liquid hits the back of my throat. Rope after rope of cum fills my mouth. I swallow again and again determined not to lose a drop.

"That's it. Take it. Take it all, baby." Tension drains from his face as his dick softens while I lick him clean. Pulling me into his arms, he cups my cheeks in his hands and kisses me with a tenderness that wraps my heart in warmth. "Thank you. That was a gift I'll treasure."

"You're welcome." I run my tongue around his lips. "Can you taste yourself?"

He tilts his head to the side. "Nope. I guess you'll have to do it again."

"Anytime, Sir," I whisper. My words are sincere. Pleasuring him stirs emotions in me I can't quite understand.

"You're not planning on going home tonight. Are you?"

"Nobody is expecting me. I can stay if you'd like."

"I'd like that very much." Zack turns off the lamp, picks up the covers, lies on his side behind me, and pulls the sheet over us. He spoons me tightly with his hand cupping my breast. I fall asleep tucked against his strong warm body.

I wake to sunlight streaming in through the windows and his hard-on is pressed between my butt cheeks. I wiggle against him but he doesn't move, so I slide out of bed and run to the bathroom.

A look in the mirror is a shocker. Mascara has smeared under my eyes and my hair looks as if Zack tied it in knots. I dig around in a drawer until I find a comb and work the tangles out. After washing my face with soap that smells like him and brushing my teeth with his toothpaste on my finger, I'm wide awake when I crawl back into bed. He's rolled onto his back so I rest my head on his shoulder and swing my leg over his.

"Hmm." He snuggles me closer. "You smell good. Did you shower without me?"

"No. I washed my face with your soap." I move my leg up and over his erection. Just feeling his bare skin sends moisture between my legs.

His hand tangles in my hair. "Best first date ever," he whispers.

"I have a confession. It usually takes more than one date to get me in bed, but last night was different. It felt special. Like more than just sex."

Zack's silence stuns me. Shit, I've said too much. Maybe last night was enough for him. Maybe it's better this way. Maybe after a few weeks, it won't hurt anymore.

Sure, I'll spend a few nights feeling the pain of rejection, but I'll get past it and appreciate the experience for what it was, the best sex of my life. Chels and Kayla will bring me food, wine, and comfort. I will survive if it ends here.

Embarrassed I've admitted last night was special, I slide out of bed and move away from him. "Want some coffee?"

Before he can see my embarrassment, I turn my back and walk toward the stairs bare-footed and bare-assed.

"Sure." The sheets rustle behind me. Shit, he's getting up. "I'll help."

"No," I snap a little too harshly. "Stay in bed and I'll bring it to you."

"Bathroom first."

I wait on the stairway until the door closes behind him and then run back for my dress and shoes. The Keurig makes Zack his cup of coffee while I slide on my dress and fasten it. My strappy red shoes look odd on my feet at nine in the morning, but they'll carry me out of here.

I don't need to hear how last night wasn't "different" to Zack, so I'll say goodbye and call an Uber to take me home. I take a deep breath, walk into the bedroom, and pretend he's not the sexiest, most gorgeous man I've ever seen. He's propped up on the pillows with an expression on his face that looks like he'd bite me if I got too close. I refuse to act like my leaving is a big deal.

"Why are you dressed?"

"I don't know if you use cream or sugar, but it's hot." I place his cup on the bedside table, hold my shoulders straight, and make an effort to appear calm. "Stay put. I'll call an Uber."

Zack's hand grips my wrist. "I asked you a question and I expect you to answer me. You're upset, so talk to me."

I shrug, trying to extricate my arm, yet have no luck. "In case you haven't noticed it's daylight. The date is over, and I don't think I'll stick around for the 'it's not you, it's me' speech."

Chapter 4

Zack

She thought I was going to blow her off? "Take off that fucking dress and get back in bed before I rip it off and paddle your sweet ass."

"Why?" Her jaw is set like she's ready for a fight, but her eyes give her away. An abandoned kitten on the side of the highway couldn't look more hurt and confused.

"You don't get to ask. Remember? My rules? You trust me to make the right choices for you and I choose to have you naked in my bed." I don't raise my voice. I've found dropping it an octave or two makes a bigger impact. At the same time, my chest feels as if a grenade exploded inside me.

Morgan's blue eyes are dark as an angry sea but she obeys my command, letting her dress fall to the floor. I swing my feet off the bed and pull her onto my lap. "Feet." Her body is stiff as I slide off her shoes one at a time. I stand and lift her in my arms and place her in the center of my bed.

She still hasn't spoken a word, so I crawl on top of her so we're skin to skin. I can't find words for the emotions I'm feeling, so I kiss her. I breathe a sigh of relief when she opens her mouth and allows my tongue inside. Passion ignites between us, turning our kiss into a duel of tongues while our hands roam across bare flesh.

Her soft moan releases the rest of the tension in my body. My cock is hard as steel and I can't help but smile.

"What made you think I wanted you to leave?" I shift so she can feel my erection pressing against her thigh. "If I had my way, you'd spend the day in my bed with my cock buried inside you."

"You have an amazing depth for romantic words." Her eyes return to sparkling blue, and her sexy smile makes me want her even more.

"That's me. I'm a real charmer." I try joking but fail. "One who wants you to stay."

"Truth or lie?" Her eyebrows lift. I like this playful side of her. My cock agrees as it swells even larger.

"Lie and truth," I admit. "I haven't charmed you this morning. I almost let you slip away. But I need the truth from you."

"You clammed up the minute I said our time together felt like more."

I can't dispute my reaction. The truth stunned me. "I'll admit hearing you say it out loud threw me for a second." I cup her cheeks in my hands and brush my lips over hers. "You're also right. I'm just not accustomed to having such a good start in a relationship. In fact, I've been avoiding one for a long time."

"Thank you for being honest." Morgan relaxes into me. "Your coffee is getting cold. Want me to make you a fresh cup?"

"I don't need caffeine to wake me up if you're in my bed." She squeals when I lift her and roll onto my back, sitting her on top of me. I slip my hand between us and spread her outer lips, but don't sink into her. Instead, I catch her hips and settle her open pussy over the length of my cock.

"Oh, I love this." Morgan rubs back and forth, sliding the head of my cock across her clit. She leans forward and watches. "You're very good at this."

Shit, she's beautiful with her hair flowing in a curtain around her cheeks. I hold back my desire to slam into her until I've covered my cock with protection. I have to show her how badly I want her here with me.

She smiles down at me with mischief filled eyes. "Are you going to do something now that the condom is on?"

"I'm going to fuck you until your pussy is sore." I lift her so she can guide me inside her wet heat. With one thrust, I impale her and pound into her just as she wanted. She fits me like a handmade glove that only I can wear.

She catches my gaze and changes pace, riding me and rubbing her clit against my pubic bone. "You feel so good inside me."

"You should feel it from my side." I shove her hair to one side and reach for her breasts. "Look how your nipples get hard for me even before I touch them." I pinch and pull on her nipples until she groans.

"I wonder what causes that." Morgan's eyes are filled with desire.

"Come here." I catch the back of her neck and pull her face to mine. Our lips crash, tongues dance, and I relish her taste. Morgan captures my bottom lip in her mouth and sucks. I can't hold back much longer.

With my hands on her hips, I guide her as she lifts up and down, fucking herself with my dick. Sweat covers our bodies, but neither of us cares. Our movements are pushing us both closer to the edge. Pulling her down on the base of my dick, I grind my hips until her head falls back, and she tightens around me.

"Zack," she cries. "I'm going to come."

"I've got you. Come on my cock. Come." My groan mingles with Morgan's and fills the room. Her back bows, body jerks, and she pulses around me. I keep grinding, milking every drop of cum out of her until she drops onto my chest. I explode, emptying myself into the condom buried deep inside her.

I gently roll us to our sides and cup her face in my hand. Her chest and cheeks are rosy with the afterglow of her orgasm. The contented smile on her face is a look I want to keep there. Her trust shakes my very foundation.

"It's never been easy for me to orgasm especially not vaginally. You've ruined me."

"I hope so. I've never seen anything more beautiful than you when you come. You were born for me."

"You just might be right."

"Next time we'll work on multiple orgasms."

"That may turn out to be a chore for you."

"Challenge accepted. I hate to get out of bed and leave the comfort of your warm body, but I don't have a choice. My crew will be at the club this afternoon. After a Friday night, there's work to be done before we open."

"Then you'd better shower or you'll smell like sex for the rest of the day."

"I'm not sure I object to smelling like you." I sit up, swing my feet to the floor, quickly remove and tie off the condom. "How about we shower then I'll fix you breakfast?"

"Heaven help me. You fuck like a god and cook too?"

"Stay there for a minute." I laugh at her wicked humor. "Reserve your judgment until you've tasted my scrambled eggs." I walk to my bathroom and drop the condom in the trash bin. I turn on the shower, wet a towel, and carry it to the bedroom. Morgan reaches for it but I shake my head. "Nope. I take care of you, remember?"

"Sorry, Sir." She grins as her legs spread wide giving me a clear picture of her pussy still wet with her juices.

Shit, I'm hard again. "You're going to be the death of me." I crawl between her legs and slowly wash her.

"It's your fault." She lifts her hips so I can slide the towel under her. "You bring out the lust in me."

I pull her off the bed, into a deep kiss, then turn her toward the bathroom. "Let's get in the shower before I feed you something besides food."

I step into the steam right behind her. She changes places with me, putting me directly under the rain showerhead. Her fingernails run up my chest to my shoulders, and I realize she's grabbed the bar of soap.

"My turn to take care of you."

"Jesus." I close my eyes and let her coat my body with suds. By the time she cups my balls in her hand, I'm as hard as a brick.

"Hold this please." She puts the soap in my hand and slowly sinks to her knees and washes my cock until I'm moaning. "Step back and rinse off, Sir."

Water sluices over the top of my head, down my shoulders, and between my legs. Her hands are still massaging my balls when she wraps her mouth around me. Her moan sends vibrations up my spine. "Fuck," I gasp. The sound echoes off the shower walls.

She slips my cock out of her mouth and licks the tip. "Do we have time for this?"

"We'll make time." I fist her hair and hang on for the ride. She runs the flat of her tongue up the underside of my dick then laps the precum off the tip. Her dark eyes remain on my face when she takes me to the back of her throat and sucks me deep. "Enough." I pull her hair. "I'm going to come."

Morgan shakes her head and digs her fingers into my ass.

"Ahhhh, God. Take me deep." My orgasm hits in a torrent, pulse after pulse of cum shoots down her throat. My legs are weak when I pull her onto her feet, into my arms, and hold her against my chest. She'd gotten inside my head and under my skin a hell of a lot faster than anyone ever has. I'm not sure if it's a good thing or not, but I want to keep her. The kiss I give her takes the place of the many things I should say. She wraps her arms around my waist and rests her head on my chest.

"I'm starving." Morgan's stomach growls emphasizing her statement. "I'll finish in here if you'll fix breakfast.

"I'll go, but no orgasms. That's my pleasure to give."

"Yes, Sir." Morgan's lips curl downward into a pout. "Not without you."

Her breasts are too beautiful to ignore so I slide my hands under them, lift, and one at a time, suck her nipples into my mouth for only a second or two. "There's only one reason I'd leave these beauties and that's because you're hungry. You'll find clean T-shirts in the bottom drawer of the chest." I dry off and add a parting thought. "Or you can come just as you are."

"I'll find something. Go. Cook."

I slide on a pair of warm-ups and hustle downstairs. Technically, it's lunchtime, but it doesn't take long to have bacon in the frying pan and eggs in a bowl ready to whip. The sound of her footsteps on the stairs alerts me that Morgan will join me soon. The eggs are cooking when she steps behind me and slips her arms around my waist.

"Smells wonderful. What can I do to help?"

"You can make the coffee." I nod at a cabinet door. "You know where the cups are and the dishes are in the same cupboard. You'll find silverware in the drawer closest to your beautiful ass."

Morgan wiggles her butt against mine and then sets the table. She opens the fridge and grabs orange juice and jelly while I drop bread into the toaster.

Toast buttered, I put the eggs and bacon on two plates and joined her. After we're seated, she lifts her coffee, leans over the cup and breathes deeply.

"We work well as a team." Steam from her cup drifts up, caressing her face.

"That's true. Eat up." I don't try to hold back my smile when she digs in like she's starving. Morgan doesn't have an ounce of fat on her body and, apparently, has a well functioning metabolism. "You're sexy as hell in the shirt I wore last night but you can have a clean one."

"I like this one. It smells like you."

"I can't argue with that." I take our cups and refill them. It occurs to me that she looks comfortable at my table and, somehow, that doesn't bother me in the least. She leans back and studies me. I thought I was learning her expressions, but now I'm not so sure. "What's on your mind?"

Chapter 5

Morgan

Do I want to push him for more personal facts? He hasn't shared a lot of information, but I'd like to know the man who is quickly earning a special place in my heart. "May I ask you a few questions?"

"I don't see why not." He holds his cup to his lips and blows on the steaming coffee. "After the past twelve hours, there shouldn't be any secrets between us."

"Oh, you have secrets?" I mimic his movements with my coffee cup, smiling at him over the rim.

"None I'm not willing to share with you. What would you like to know?"

"How did you decide to be a partner in three nightclubs when you already owned a successful business?" I fork a bite of eggs into my mouth and wait. "I'm sure you have things you'd like to know about me."

"I can think of a lot of things I'd rather be doing with my mouth than strolling down memory lane." Zack's tongue peeks out and brushes across his lower lip.

I feel my neck getting warm. "Me too, but I haven't finished my breakfast."

"Okay, let's do this. You first. How old are you and where's home?"

His questions are not what I expect, but I have no reason not to be honest. "I'm twenty-eight, my sign is Gemini, and I'm a Texan, Austin to be exact. You already know about my grandmother.

"I attended Northeastern Illinois University on a partial academic scholarship. I never wanted to be a hardship on her so I worked part-time in a coffee shop to help pay my expenses. During my junior and senior year, I landed a part-time job at Slatler Advertising Firm that paid a small stipend. They offered me a full-time position as an administrative assistant to the VP of accounting when I graduated. I accepted because the pay was good and I would be able to help Nana. She wasn't in the best of health and there was no way I was leaving town. Besides, I felt at home here and wanted to stay.

"I've never been in love, although I thought so once." I pause and reflect for a moment. "It hurt that I wasn't enough woman to keep him satisfied.

"Sorry, I have a tendency to overshare. Your turn. What's your story?"

Zack's gaze drops to his coffee and for a minute I think he's not going to tell me anything. "I'm thirty-four, have no idea what my 'sign' is, and I was born in Manhattan, where I joined the Marines, which my father had always demanded I not do. He thought his son, who shared his name and maybe, someday his money, should stay home and learn to run the family business. He'd made his fortune the hard way and believed he didn't owe this country any devotion. We fought a lot about that. Dad still believes I joined the Marines just to piss him off."

Zack stands, gathers the dishes, rinses, and puts them in the dishwasher. I think he's through talking but he surprises me by coming back to the table and joining me.

"I met Nick and Slider in the military, and Nick brought me home, here, for Christmas once. It's a great town so I moved here after I left the military. I majored in Economics at the University of Chicago.

"I, too, thought I was in love once but was wrong. We divorced and she's remarried." Zack lifts his cup and drains what has to be cold coffee in one gulp. "And that's a hell of a lot more than most people know about me."

"I'm glad you formed the partnership."

"Oh, yeah? Why?"

"Gloss led me to you."

"It certainly did. I'll be sure to thank them." He pulls me into his arms and pushes me against the counter. "Did you tell anybody you were going to a member's only club.

"No. My friends are happy if I am. We tell each other everything." I think about that for a second. "Maybe I won't share as much as I used to."

"Tell them whatever you like. I don't want you to be ashamed or embarrassed by anything we do; I'm not. I have to ask, why aren't you seeing someone?"

"How do you know I'm not?"

"You don't strike me as the type of woman who would screw around on someone you're dating."

My heart squeezes. "That's one of the sweetest things I've ever been told." I stand. "I don't know if this is allowed, but may I kiss you?"

"We're not in the club or the bedroom, so, yes, you may kiss me whenever you wish." Zack opens his arms. I crave his body close to mine and I don't hesitate. I walk straight to him and slide my hands around his neck.

His lips are soft and warm as I cover them with mine. His arms tighten around me, holding me against his chest. I step down off my tiptoes and lean back. Zack's eyes are melting me from the inside out. "Better finish up here."

He catches my hand as I turn. "Do not tell anybody I said something 'sweet' to you. You'll ruin my reputation at the club."

"Yes, Sir." I take my seat again while choking back a laugh. "As far as romantic attachments, I've been on vacation from men, until I met you."

"Somebody hurt you?" His lips drew into a hard line.

"Not physically. It was more mental. My friend, Chels, never liked him. She realized my self-worth had hit bottom before I did."

"Chels?"

"Chelsea but friends call her Chels."

"Chelsea sounds like a smart woman. I'd like to meet her because your bastard ex needs his ass kicked. I think I'd enjoy working with her on that particular job."

"You wouldn't dare." I can't help but laugh.

"No. Unless he shows up in your life again. His loss is my gain, every beautiful inch of you. Unfortunately, I have business I have to attend to today, otherwise, I'd throw you over my shoulder and we'd spend the day in bed."

"Another time." I wanted the words back as soon as I said them. I don't want to sound needy.

"Would you like to go back to Silken tonight?"

There's nothing I'd rather do more than explore my fantasies with him, yet, I know to protect my heart. Falling for Zack could result in me being shattered into a thousand tiny pieces. I realize he's looking at me, waiting for an answer.

He strokes my cheek with the back of his hand. "I'll be honest with you, Morgan, I don't know what we're doing here. I can't guarantee a lifetime or even a month. All I know is that I want to see where this takes us. I need more of you."

"I . . . I would like that."

"Good. Gabriel will pick you up at nine tonight. Be ready."

"Will I interfere with your work?"

"No. I'm going to Silken this afternoon. I'll make sure my desk is clear. Nick will be there to handle any issues that arise. Nothing will keep me away from you for very long."

"That makes me happy."

"I believe it does." Zack's laugh is the most freeing sound I've ever heard. "Your eyes are sparkling like Christmas lights." He turns me and smacks my ass. "We should get going."

"If you're going to Silken, my apartment is in the opposite direction. Let me call Uber and save you some time."

"Morgan, that's not happening. I have time for you."

We head upstairs and finish dressing. Zack pulls on his watch and then pauses to stare at me. "My God, woman, you are beautiful."

"Why, thank you, Sir." I curtsy. "Even in this wrinkled old dress?"

"In or out of any dress." He escorts me out to his car, gets us both buckled in, and drives to the freeway. Zack rests his open palm on the console and I twine my fingers through his. The small squeeze I get tells me he's pleased. He parks in my apartment lot and holds my hand as we walk up the stairs to my door.

"I'd better get out of here before I forget work and we go inside to try out your bed."

"You're so full of it." He won't like it if I tell him how adorable his dimple is when he smiles so I roll my eyes.

"You think? Keeping my eyes off you while you put that black dress back on was difficult as hell. My dick has a mind of its own and it wants you. I had to wedge my erection into these slacks."

My gaze travels down to the hard swell of his cock. God, how I want to drop to my knees and pleasure him right here in front of the entire complex. I step into his arms, stand on my toes, and kiss him. "What would you like me to wear? I don't know how a typical sub dresses."

"Her dom sets those standards."

"I repeat. What would you like me to wear?"

"Something tight that shows off your beautiful body, especially your breasts. I'll send a car to pick you up at four o'clock and take you to the right boutique. They'll be expecting you and will have a few outfits selected for you to try on." He holds his hand up to stop me from speaking. "You gave me control."

I probably should've expected him to control what I wear to the club. "I'm sorry. It's been a long time since I've had anyone take care of me."

"Get used to it." He crushes me against his chest, bends and kisses my forehead. "There's no limit on outfits. Bring home as many as you like."

"Zack," I start to protest and receive his "don't argue" raised eyebrow.

"I'll see you tonight."

A shot of adrenaline rushes through me as I watch him walk down the stairs. Am I ready for this? Is this lifestyle what has been missing in every other relationship I've had?

I turn and walk into my apartment without looking back. I kick off my shoes, change into a pair of shorts, and my favorite tank top. There's more to Zack's lifestyle and I want to know about it. I grab my laptop and get comfortable. Once I've Googled Doms and subs, I discover more blogs than I could've imagined. To say I was surprised at some of the bondage equipment is an understatement. Concentrating on the submissive requirements, I fill my brain with the terminology, required behavior, and expectations of the Dom. I log off, collapse on the bed, and stare at the ceiling while committing some of what I read to memory. It's only then that I realize I'm smiling.

The sound of someone knocking startles me. It's then I realize I'd fallen asleep. I hurry to the living room and look out the peephole. I pull open the door and step back as Chels and Kayla push past me in a rush. Of course, they're dying to hear about my date.

"Morgan, you look like shit." Chels is lovely, with flawless skin, and chestnut hair, but she has no filter when it comes to speaking her mind.

Kayla, blessed with blonde hair, blue eyes, and a perfect figure, flops down on my couch. "No, she doesn't. Morgan looks like a freshly fucked woman." Kayla's filter isn't much better. She has no problem sharing her opinion. "I've gone too long without sex so spill Morgan. We know he's hot, but is he good in bed? Is he rich? Have a big dick? A twin brother?"

I collapse on the couch and join the laughter. Chels goes to the kitchen and returns with three bottles of beer. She passes one to me and Kayla before sitting on the floor, legs folded under her. I raise my eyebrows waiting for the deluge of questions.

"Well? Don't make us beg," she says.

"Zack Pierce is amazing in and out of bed." I threw that out and let it sit for a minute. "He's sending a car at four o'clock to take me shopping for something to wear to the club tonight."

"You're moving pretty damn fast with this guy. I'll cut off his balls if he hurts you," Kayla declares, always ready to protect us.

"No." I shake my head. "Didn't you hear me say he's amazing? I can't wait to see him tonight." It occurs to me I'm not joking. I can barely hold in my excitement.

Chels scoots closer to the couch. "What's on for tonight?"

"Zack is sending a driver to pick me up at nine and take me back to his members-only club." Just talking about him makes me sweat. "We stopped by Silken last night, and I can't wait to go back."

Kayla leans close to me. "What was it like?"

"It was certainly different. Some things shocked me and some . . . intrigued me." I wait for my cheeks to heat up but nothing happens. My interest in Zack and his lifestyle doesn't embarrass me. "I'm not ashamed I went, or that I'm going again. So if you're going to lecture me, please don't. I prefer your support." I pause and wait for their reactions, relaxing when they both nod. "And I'd like you both to go shopping with me."

Kayla pumps her fist. "Damn right, I'm going. This day just keeps getting better."

Chels stands, collects our bottles, and takes them to the kitchen. "I'm ready when you are."

"I want to know more about this BDSM, members-only club." Kayla's head swiveled toward Chels.

"It's not just a BDSM club. It's a place people can explore their fantasies." I get off the couch. "We can talk on the way. I need to shower, shop, have dinner, and be ready by nine." I pull Kayla to her feet. "I expect you both to give me some credit. Nothing is going to happen without my permission."

Kayla threw her arm around my shoulders. "If you're sure this club is safe, I'm all for you enjoying life. I'm just jealous as hell."

"Let me get ready." I hurry to the bathroom and set record time getting ready. I'm curious about Chels's knowledge of women's clubwear, but I want to hear the story when we're not in a hurry.

My phone beeps and I see a text saying the car is waiting for me downstairs. The three of us head down and Chels does a low whistle when she sees the driver standing next to the limo at the curb. "Now he's what I call a classy ride."

The driver is wearing aviator sunglasses, but his blond hair and big smile are enough to convince me he's gorgeous in that black suit. He holds the door open and we pile in the back. The buttery-soft leather seats and thick pile carpeting are pure luxuries.

Kayla is stroking the armrest like it's a baby kitten. "I feel like Publisher's Clearing House just left me one of those monster checks."

We're on the highway when the driver looks in the rearview mirror and says, "There's champagne in the mini bar for your enjoyment."

After we've finished our first glass, and are working on the second, I deal with their barrage of questions about Zack and the club. I'm excited about the shop we're going to but talking about him makes me just as happy. If I want to continue our relationship—and I don't want this to end—I'll yield to his decisions. A simple conversation concerning the two of us makes my body yearn for him.

The store is located in an upscale strip mall between a walk-in medical clinic and a liquor store. The front of the store has darkened glass windows with the words The Special Touch in gold. On the door, a sign says by appointments only.

Our driver stops, gets out of the limo, and opens our door. "Take as long as you like."

I look wide-eyed at my two best friends, and it's Chels who rings the bell. When the door clicks, we march inside, united, like we're used to shopping surrounded by vibrators, whips, ball gags, blow-up dolls, and things which I have no explanation for their use.

An attractive woman wearing a barely-there, black leather skirt, a black bra under a black, see-through blouse with black stilettos meets us with a smile. "Ms. Kimball, welcome to The Special Touch Boutique. I'm Andrea, the selections Mr. Pierce chose are ready for you to try on."

"You don't get to pick your own outfit?" Kayla's pale eyebrows pull together.

"Stop frowning like that," Chels admonishes her. "This is Morgan's decision to make."

"It doesn't sound right to me." Kayla looks at me.

"Zack and I discussed this. Let's not argue."

Andrea leads me toward the back of the store. "With your figure, the outfits Mr. Pierce selected will look great on you."

"He was here?"

"Yes. Not long ago."

Just how often does Zack shop here? "So, Mr. Pierce is a regular customer?"

Andrea grins. "His card is on file, but today is the first time he's ever personally shopped."

I smile back at her. "Thanks for telling me." A calm feeling wraps around me. Zack came here just to select outfits for me. I won't disappoint him.

"She needs matching thongs, preferably the breakaway type." Chels has stopped on the vibrator aisle.

"There are undergarments in the dressing room waiting for you. Excuse me for a moment." Andrea disappears behind a curtain covered doorway.

I round the corner on the aisle where Chels is studying a pink vibrator. I can't help but laugh. "Thank God, no other customers are here or I'd send you to the car." Both my friends appear to know a lot more about this type of store than I do and I'm glad they're with me.

"Mr. Pierce selected a size seven shoe for you. Is that correct?" Andrea asks.

"That's right." My hands are a bit sweaty, and I'm a bundle of nerves.

Kayla and Chels follow as Andrea leads us to a large room in the back. "If you step up here, we'll get started."

I find myself standing on a platform facing my friends and three mirrors are behind me. They're sitting in two high-back loungers staring at the bottle of champagne on the table between them. It takes me a second to understand that some Doms probably participate in the selection of the clothes they purchased their subs.

Andrea returns with an armful of dresses and hangs them on a rack. "Ladies, please enjoy the champagne." She joins me on the platform and reaches for my top. "Let's get you out of these clothes. I'm excited to see these outfits on you."

"You guys can shop or wait in the car if you want." I stand stiff as a board while Andrea strips off my clothing. Chels and Kayla have occasionally seen me naked, but we were in the sauna at our apartment complex or changing from wet swimsuits to dry clothes. I pull in a quick breath when Andrea's knuckles brush across my breasts.

"We're okay right here," Kayla holds up her glass in a salute.

Andrea's gaze rakes my body while she holds out a thong for me to try on. "You have a beautiful figure."

"Thanks," I mumble. I can't believe I'm allowing this stranger to strip me bare and then pull a thong up over my hips.

"Let's try on the blue dress first. It's almost the same color as your eyes."

I'm not imagining that her hands touch my body more than necessary. With just a light stroke or quick touch, Andrea is discretely acquainting herself with my boobs, belly, and butt.

The dress is made of blue spandex and looks as if someone painted it on me. The back is cut low and the tight skirt barely covers my ass. The top is much like the one I'd worn last night only this one is open from the neck to the waist. One wrong move and a breast will be on display.

"Color me naked," I say, trying not to be too embarrassed.

"We saw that already." Chels smiles, convincing me both my buddies have drunk too much champagne.

"That's hot as fuck," Kayla exclaims a bit too loudly. "Is that a breakaway thong?"

I turn a slow circle, waiting for Chels to comment. "I can't imagine another dress that will hug your body better."

"You two like it?" I'm a little surprised they're so supportive of the changes I'm making in my life and it makes me love them even more.

"Yes," Kayla says. "Get that outfit."

"I agree," Andrea purrs. "Mr. Pierce particularly liked this outfit, but this isn't the only one he liked."

"How many did he select?" I'm thrilled when she points to two more dresses. It means he's planning on seeing me more than once. My chest swells with pleasure and excitement.

After two hours of shopping, we walk outside carrying all three outfits and a bag holding matching lingerie that Zack selected. I question the need for four-inch, fuck-me heels for each outfit, but they do make my legs and ass look good.

Immediately, the limo moves in our direction. The driver opens our door, takes my packages from me, and puts them upfront in the passenger seat.

I fasten my belt and speak to the driver, "I'm sorry, but I didn't catch your name."

"That's quite all right." He turns in his seat and looks back at us. "I'm Taylor Horne, Ms. Kimball.

"Thank you for waiting for us."

"My pleasure. Are you ladies ready to go home?"

"Yes," I lean back and relax for the first time in a couple of hours. Zack has more than one date in mind. Why else would he have selected more than one outfit? I can hope that's what he's planning. "The dresses are sexy, but they're so revealing."

"What?" Kayla laughs. "You have the figure for it."

"So do you."

Kayla scoffs. "I don't have a reason to wear clubwear." She pauses. "Yet."

"If Zack is pushing you to wear something you're not comfortable with, don't wear it." I can always count on Chels to be the voice of reason.

"Actually, he said I'd look great in whatever I wore."

"Then wear whatever you want." Chels pats my knee as if I'm a kid, even though we're the same age.

"You mean whatever he wants, don't you?" Kayla asked.

"Would you wear outfits like the ones Zack bought me?" I ask Kayla.

"Maybe. If I had a reason."

Chels changes the music playing on the radio system in the back of the limo. Finally, she finds music she likes and takes a deep breath. "It's been a fun holiday so far."

"And it's not over." I can't help but gloat.

The driver stops in front of our apartment building and opens our door. He offers to carry my packages upstairs, but between the three of us, we can manage.

Before I can thank him, Chels steps in front of me.

"Thank you, Taylor. We appreciate your time."

"My pleasure," he repeats. But this time his gaze locks on Chels for a minute before he drives away.

"Did you just flirt with our driver?" I chuckle. "He certainly had eyes for you."

Chels shrugs her shoulder and follows us up the stairs. "Don't tell me nobody noticed he was fucking hot."

"We noticed." Kayla laughs as we enter my living room. "We just weren't as obvious as you."

I take the dresses into my room and hang them in my closet. Then I join Chels and Kayla in the living room, where I check the time on my cell. "We spent two hours shopping and used up an hour on the round trip. That leaves me with two hours to shower and finish my hair and makeup."

"Which one of the outfits are you wearing?" Chels carries the last two shopping bags into my bedroom.

"Since Zack is partial to the blue dress, I'm wearing it. I've come this far and I'm not quitting. Not after the best sex, I've ever had—and hope to have again."

"Now you're talking." Kayla gives me a fist bump.

"You two stay in here." I point to the couch. "I'll show you the finished look."

As usual, Chels ignores my instructions and heads to my kitchen. "You didn't mention dinner, so I'm fixing something to eat. You can't go clubbing without having a decent meal in your belly."

I rush over and hug her. "Thanks, Mom."

The warm water in the shower eases the tension in my shoulders while I shampoo my hair, and then use a new razor to ensure there are no stray hairs anywhere they're not wanted. Afterward, staring in the mirror, I decide on a different hairstyle. It takes a little longer but when I finish with the blow dryer and flat iron, my wavy hair is straight, smooth, and in a high ponytail. Too much makeup feels over the top, so I keep it to a minimum except for my eyes, those I go for the bold look.

My thong is a string with a small triangle of cloth in front and two very flat pearl snaps. The challenge for me will be to not dig that string from between my butt cheeks all tonight. I step into the dress, pull it over my hips, and tie the bow at the back of my neck. With a deep breath, I turn and stand in front of my full-length mirror.

"Holy shit." Completely surprised, I stare at my reflection. The look is hot and I still haven't put on those fuck-me heels.

"Can you stop long enough to eat?" Chels calls out through the door.

"Be right there." I take a deep breath then walk into the living room. "Something smells good."

"Fuck me." Kayla's jaw looks as if it's completely unhinged.

"You like?" I do a pirouette.

"If I were into women, I'd hit that." Kayla licks her lips with a laugh.

"Kayla, you're crazy," Chels calls out from the kitchen, laughing as she joins us. Her eyes blink rapidly. "Shit. I think I agree."

Chels puts her hands on my shoulders. "I feel like a mother hen when the first chick leaves the nest. You've never flipped over a man so fast. I . . . we," she amends waving her hand back and forth between herself and Kayla, "just want you to be happy."

"It's completely against my nature to move this fast, but I have to let this play out. When Zack turns those chocolate-brown eyes on me, every cell in my body heats up."

"Then trust your gut." Kayla studies me for a second. "You are fucking stunning. That hairstyle is brilliant. And the dress? You've never looked so incredibly sexy."

"Thank you, both. I needed that boost." I open my arms and hug them. I've never loved them more than I do today. "Let's eat." I use a towel to shield my dress while I wolf down a bowl of chicken noodle soup and a grilled cheese sandwich. The combination never tasted better, and the chatter at the table keeps my mind busy for a few minutes.

"Let's get the kitchen clean." Chels stands and gathers our plates. "When we finish the dishes, we're leaving. It won't hurt you to have a minute or two alone before the driver arrives."

"Yeah," Kayla agrees. "But we expect explicit details tomorrow."

Chels takes hold of my hand. "You call if you need us for anything, at any time."

I nod and a few minutes later I watch them walk out my front door. I sink into the soft cushions on my couch well aware that if the dress weren't spandex,

I'd have to stand all night. It's short and tight but I admit to myself, the outfit is sexy as hell. Too nervous to sit still for long, I stand and pace, thinking about what tonight might bring. I don't know why I want to please Zack so badly. But I do.

I go to the bathroom, brush my teeth, and check my hair and makeup one more time. I've just slipped on my killer heels when someone knocks on my door.

Expecting the driver, my mouth drops open in surprise. "Zack," I squeal my surprise. "I'm so glad you came."

"I just couldn't send a driver." Zack leans down and captures my lips with a gentle and romantic kiss. He takes a step back and openly stares at me. "Fuck. You're stunning. We should get moving before I forget where we're going."

"Thank you. I'm so glad you like the new look. I've never been called stunning."

"Then the men in your life have been fools. I have more documents for you to read and sign before we go to the club." His face is unreadable. No grin. No sparkle. My mouth instantly goes dry, making my throat feel raspy. He reaches inside his suit jacket and pulls out a couple of folded sheets of paper.

"As long as you're with me, there's no application to fill out. These are a little different than the ones you signed before. The second document is for you to read and identify sexual situations and/or acts you're willing or unwilling to participate in with me. There's also an explanation of the green, yellow, and red safe words. The last page is the nondisclosure form."

I take the papers from him and sit at my breakfast bar. Unnerved as hell, I try for a little humor. "Where's your page of things you will and will not do?"

Zack leans over and whispers in my ear. "There's nothing I won't do if it pleases you." A chill races up my spine when he places a pen next to my hand, moves to my couch, and casually thumbs through a magazine.

I understand and agree that nothing I do or observe at the club can be made public. I appreciate the anonymity too, so I sign and date it before moving to the next document. Heat burns up my neck as I read the activities possible. Shit. There are a lot of things on this list I've never experienced. I roll the pen in my fingers as my brain spins. Just how serious am I? The time has come to make a decision. Under the no column, I check a few items such as golden showers, scat play, which makes my stomach turn over, and fisting. The pen hovers over spankings with assorted objects, the use of ball gags, ropes, anal play, and anal sex to name a few examples. I glance over at Zack, and his gaze meets mine as if he expected me to look his way. I want him more than I've ever wanted a man. I feel alive with him. Somehow, most of the acts listed don't frighten me.

I read the definition of the safe words, agree I will follow all the club rules without question, and then carry the signed pages to Zack.

Using some of the knowledge I gained while researching, I try out a position. Presenting for him, I stand with my feet shoulder-width apart, arms clasped behind my back, and my gaze on the floor in front of me. "If it pleases you, Sir, I'm ready to leave."

"I see you've done more homework. I'm proud of you." He stands and lifts my chin with his fingers. "I prefer you to look at me when we talk. Someday, I might ask you to take the submissive position at the club. But tonight, I want you to relax."

"I will." Deep inside I realize my life is about to undergo radical changes and I can't wait. "May I kiss you, Sir?"

"Since you put that in the form of a question." The spark is back in his eyes and he crushes me against his chest. Our lips are almost touching when he whispers, "I'm glad you signed the papers. Your strength and bravery make me very proud." The kiss is soft, hinting at greater rewards in the near future. "By the way, I wasn't kidding. You are stunning."

"You honestly like the outfit?" I know I'm fishing for compliments, but his approval is important to me. I want that more than anything.

"I love it. I knew you'd look hot as hell in this dress." He slides his fingers inside the opening between my breasts and my nipples instantly pebble. I love it when his hands are on me. "Hmm, easy off."

"Of course." My heart is pounding hard enough for Zack to see my carotid pulsing. He drops his head under my jaw and kisses his way down the vein throbbing in my neck. His hands slide under the hem of my dress and caress my bare butt cheeks. Moisture pools, soaking my tiny thong and I know Zack realizes it. I want him with an almost scary passion and I'm not turning away from him. He makes me feel desired, protected, and beautiful. That's something I've never felt and I admit it makes me light-headed.

A low growl rolls out of him. It sounds as if it came from deep in his chest. "You're beyond sexy. This dress is enough to make me crazy, and the ponytail, shit, I want to wrap it around my hand and hold on tight while I fuck you until you scream my name."

His face is glowing as he releases me and walks a circle around me. The fingertips of one hand brush against my body as he moves. I can see the monster bulge in his slacks. He catches my hand, rubbing it up and down his erection.

"See how you affect me? As much as I'd like to throw you over my shoulder and carry you to bed, I won't. Walking into the club with you at my side, looking the way you do right now, hell, I can't wait to show you to my world."

Zack slips a black cape he purchased for me around my shoulders before extending his arm. His muscles tighten in my grip. I look up at him and search his masculine, yet beautiful face. "Thank you. I needed to hear that."

"Get used to it, because you'll hear it again at the club." He escorts me to a huge, black SUV and helps me into the back seat before sliding in next to me. "Our appointments for blood tests are scheduled for noon this coming Monday. I'll text you the address. The doctor is a friend and will expedite the results. I'm impatient to be inside you, skin to skin."

I can only nod. "Me too."

"Morgan, you remember Gabriel. He and Taylor are the only people I will ever send for you."

Gabriel nods without looking back.

The ride out of town to Silken goes by quickly while I tell Zack about my adventure to The Right Touch and Andrea's touchy fingers. Zack's laughter fills me, lifts my spirits, and I'm so happy to be with him.

Gabriel stops at the front door and Zack helps me out of the SUV. He takes my cape when we reach the outer doors. His gaze sweeps over my body again, stopping at my eyes. "I'm proud as hell to walk beside you tonight. Fair warning, I might get a little jealous too. Maybe I need to get two white ribbons for you to wear."

I stand there stunned and thrilled at his praise. "You don't mind if I like that you're jealous, do you?"

"I prefer it." His smile beams down at me, giving me a flash of his dimple. "I'm going to stay hard all night."

My hand rubs the front of his slacks. "I prefer it."

"Brave girl." He turns me and smacks my bottom before reaching around me and opening the door. I can't help but laugh at his playfulness.

"That's the first time I've ever been spanked."

Zack leans into me. His warm breath floats past my ear. "I think you liked that," he whispers.

My face heats as I realize Gabriel has walked past us, unseen, and is watching with a grin that's spread across his face. He's quite handsome when he smiles. Gabriel signs me in and then places a white ribbon on my arm. "Have a pleasant evening."

"You must have a twin," I say wondering how he got from the car to the front desk so quickly. "How else can you be two places at once?"

Gabriel looks down at me. "You caused quite a stir last night but tonight . . ."

"Yes?" Zack lifts an eyebrow pretending to question Gabriel's next response.

"Tonight you're even lovelier."

"You're too kind." I resist the temptation to kiss him on his cheek. It's probably too early in the friendship for that.

He opens the interior door, and Zack escorts me inside. His hand rests low on my back and his thumb caresses my spine.

"I'll introduce you to my manager, Danielle, she was off last night. She's worked here since we opened and knows this place and how it ticks better than any of us. I couldn't do without her."

The bartender says something to a woman at the bar. She spins on the stool, stands, and pulls her long, red hair over one shoulder. Tall with a slender body, she has perfect hourglass curves. She smoothes her hand over her black pencil skirt, adjusts the open collar on her white blouse, and walks toward us. At least four buttons are undone, showing her ample cleavage shift as she moves. My heart sinks. She's stunning and her eyes are locked on Zack. Feeling territorial, I move closer to him.

"You didn't have to hurry back," she says. "I have everything under control."

"No doubt. Morgan, this is Danielle."

I extend my hand and she meets me for a handshake. "Nice to meet you. Zack's been telling me how much he depends on you." Danielle's important to him and I don't want her to dislike me.

"Nice to meet you too. If he's been bragging, now might be a good time for me to ask for a raise." Danielle laughs and turns to Zack. "I hate to interrupt your night but I need your signature on a couple of applications. If you do this now, I won't bother you two again and I can have the background checks started first thing tomorrow."

Zack hesitates; his arm tightens around my waist. No way would I keep him from his business. "Go. I'm a big girl."

"That's what worries me." His lips touch mine. "I won't take long."

A full-body shiver washes over me while they walk away. Several men watch the sway of her hips, but she doesn't recognize their interest. I wonder if Danielle is a sub or a domme.

Noise from farther back in the club draws my attention so I take a few steps down the first aisle to watch the open scenes.

I see a naked woman bound to a table with her arms stretched over her head and her legs splayed open. Two men stand on either side of the table stroking their limp cocks. They release the restraints and she stretches out onto a padded bench. Cum is spread across her breasts and stomach. Dipping in two fingers, she draws patterns and moves it around as if it were body art. She scoops the cum up with two fingers and licks them clean. She repeats the process again and again. It's not surprising that both men are as hard as steel again. Her face is aglow with pleasure when I walk away.

Someone grabs my arm and spins me around. "What the fuck are you doing here?"

My stomach drops to the floor. The last person on earth I expect to see is Dale Loften, who's snarling at me like a mad dog. Feeling no fear, I glare at him. "What I do is none of your business. We've been over for months."

"We're leaving, Morgan. Now. You don't belong here."

"I'm not going anywhere with you." I jerk my arm trying to break away, but he squeezes harder. "Take your hands off me."

"Look at you dressed like a slut. You were hiding a secret from me all the time we were together." His skin-crawling gaze rakes my body. "My dick is harder than it ever was when we fucked. I like this side of you. Your eyes sparkled when that sub scooped their cum up with her fingers and put it in her mouth. I'm going to give you another chance."

"That's not happening."

His grip tightens. "Now, baby, don't be so negative, your dirty little secret is safe with me."

"Leave me alone before I scream for help."

Dale's face darkens. "Have you been here before?"

His spittle hits my cheek and I feel the need for a hot shower. "That's none of your business. Go away and stay the fuck out of my life."

"Like hell, I will." His face comes closer to mine.

"You try to kiss me and I'll bite off your lip."

For a second I think he's going to hit me, instead, he growls. "If you're a sexual submissive, why did you hide it from me? I put up with vanilla sex for months, when all along you were a pain slut. I'm going to train you to be my perfect slave."

"No, Dale. I've moved on and so should you." I look back toward Zack's office. I don't want to cause a scene but I'm getting ready to scream.

"Oh, no, baby, we've just begun."

Just then, the tension tying me in knots relaxes as Zack walks into my line of sight. At first, he starts walking to where he left me, but then he stops, scans the room until his gaze catches mine. There's no doubt he can see my fear because he covers the distance between us in seconds. His eyes are hard and his lips are drawn into a thin line. He holds my gaze until he stops and turns that intense glare on Dale.

"Take your fucking hands off her." Zack's low, gritty tone sends shivers down my spine. "Come here, Morgan."

"Yes, Sir." Dale's grip on my arm quickly releases.

Zack's arm comes around my waist pulling me close. "You can clearly see the lady is wearing a white ribbon." His possessiveness sends pride streaming through my veins. His eyes have darkened to black coal. "You're done here."

Dale lifts his hands in surrender. "I wasn't asking her to scene with me. We're old friends."

"I don't give a fuck who you are. You don't put your hands on Morgan or anyone in my club without permission." Zack catches my chin and lifts my head. "You know this piece of shit?"

"I know him, but we're not friends by any stretch." I rub the spot on my arm where Dale's hand left red fingerprints, then I snuggle closer to Zack. His fist winds my ponytail around his fingers as he glares at Dale.

"What's your name?" Zack's tone leaves no doubt he's furious that Dale had his hands on me.

"Dale Loften." His voice has turned meek, uncertain as he glances around the room as if looking for someone. "I should find my friends."

"You have five minutes to find them and get out or I'll help you."

Dale scurries off toward the back of the building. Zack looks like he wants to kill Dale. I've never witnessed this side of him and it makes me proud, yet a little uneasy. I run my thumb over the stubble on his chin. "Sir, may I ask you to kiss me? Please."

His eyes crinkle at the corners as he smiles. He yanks me against his chest and his lips crash down on mine. His hands cup my ass and lift my feet off the floor while our tongues plunder each other's mouths. When we separate, we're both panting as if we just finished running a marathon.

"Did that bastard hurt you?" Zack's composure has returned. How he masters control of his emotions so fast is incredibly sexy.

"No. I'm fine. I should have stayed where you left me."

"What did he say to you?" His dark eyes seem to see right through me. "Don't lie to me."

"He asked me why I was here."

"And?" Obviously, Zack isn't ready to drop the subject of Dale.

"He wanted to know why I hadn't shown my submissive side when we dated." I grip Zack's arm and smile up at him. "I didn't tell Dale it's because he's not you. Please, don't let him ruin our night."

"If the son of a bitch left a bruise on you, he'll see just how I feel about anyone fucking with you."

"He startled me more than anything.

"I'll make sure Gabriel escorts him out." Zack pulls his cell out and speaks softly into the phone. A few seconds later, Gabriel steps inside and walks straight to where we're standing.

"Are you okay?" Gabriel's nostrils are flared. He almost looks happy he's about to throw someone out.

"I'm fine. I don't want to cause a scene."

"None of this is your fault. He broke the rules by putting his hands on you." Zack's index finger caresses the white ribbon on my bicep. "He saw that you belonged to someone." His demeanor changes; the muscles in his jaw relax.

"That's him talking to two men in front of the open scene. He's the blond wearing a white shirt with no jacket," I tell Gabriel.

"On it."

"Maybe the white ribbon isn't enough. A collar around your neck would be more obvious," Zack whispers in my ear.

"I've noticed a few members wear leather colors." I lean against him, breathing in his clean scent. "Would you expect me to wear it to work?"

"No, and, as much as I like leather, you need something more feminine." Zack winks at me, takes my hand, and leads me back to the front of the club. He stops where the lighting is better and rakes his lusty gaze over my body, scorching my skin. "We have tonight and Sunday to enjoy ourselves."

I sigh as relief hits me. "You made plans for the weekend?"

"No set plans, but I'm not letting anything ruin this for you." He slips his hand inside the slit in the front of my dress, brushing my nipple with the back of his hands. "I can't wait to watch you undress for me."

"I can't wait to take these shoes off. Did you choose them to torture my feet?"

Zack's laugh sounds as if it comes from deep in his chest. It's the first time I've heard that hard of a laugh from him and my insides almost melt. "Let's find a booth and I'll take them off you right now."

"No way. They make my legs look sexy as hell."

"That they do. You're fucking smoldering hot. The thought of you wearing nothing but those shoes in a scene with me demonstrating how to make a woman come using just my tongue is driving me crazy."

I laugh, not feeling a bit of embarrassment. "I can't believe how much I've changed in just two short days."

"Do tell." Evil flames light his eyes. "Exactly how much have you changed?"

"Well." I lift up on my toes to whisper in his ear. "The idea of a demonstration doesn't scare me. It sounds hot and interesting."

"Truth or lie?" He's so gorgeous when his dark eyes fill with lust.

"Truth."

"That's my brave girl." Zack cups my cheeks and kisses me again, claiming me for everyone to see. "Let's take that walk."

Chapter 6

Zack

Deep breaths do nothing to slow my heart rate or ease my need to kick Loften's ass. Seeing that bastard with his hand on Morgan made me want to pummel him and break my own club rule of no fighting and kick his ass out the front door. I still might if he's left bruises on her body. Nobody fucking touches what's mine. That bastard is in her past and he will stay there.

"Let's start the night again." We pick a booth close to the bar. "Would you like a drink?"

"Hmm, maybe a glass of red wine." Morgan crosses her legs. They're a feast for my eyes.

"This dress wasn't designed for sitting." I pat the space between us and she swings her legs toward me and away from curious eyes.

"Inside these walls, you're allowed to flaunt your beauty with pride." I give our order to the waitress and ask that Danielle be located and sent to our booth.

"Everyone who works here is gorgeous."

"You think so?" I joke.

"Especially you."

I stroke my hand up her smooth legs, betting she took extra care getting ready for me. Morgan shifts and half her breast is on display just enough to make my mouth water.

Danielle approaches, carrying our drinks. She drops napkins in place then sits our drinks in front of us. "You wanted to see me?"

"Yes," I speak softly to ensure privacy. "Dale Loften is barred for life. Along with his friends who brought him as their guest." I hate knowing that bastard has been inside Morgan's body, and tonight I'll do my best to erase those memories.

Unless he hurt her. Then I'll make it my business to inflict pain on that motherfucker in ways he's never imagined.

"You got it." Danielle nods at Morgan and walks away.

We sit in silence for a while, Morgan sipping her wine, and me drinking Irish whiskey. I push my hand past her knee and she turns to face me. Her eyes are glazed as if she's deep into the scenes around us. How her simple look of lust can affect me so fast is a little disconcerting. I shift, trying to find room for my growing erection.

Morgan's character goes a lot deeper than just her outer beauty. The way she treated the wait staff at the restaurant and my team here at the club speaks volumes about her heart. She exudes warmth, kindness, humility, and innocence. My brain stopped on the word innocence. As badly as I want to tie her down and spank her sexy ass, I have to offer her a way out.

"Would you like to finish our drinks and go? I haven't shown you around Gloss or Gallants yet."

"I'd like to stay here." Her gaze drifts to one of the scenes.

"I don't want to rush you."

"I don't feel rushed. I feel excited." She licks her bottom lip, and I immediately change my mind. I stand and reach out to her, watching her small hand disappear into mine.

"Walk with me."

"Yes, Sir." She stands without looking up, keeping her gaze on her shoes.

"Eyes up this time," I whisper in her ear then catch the tip and bite down. She flinches, laughs, and leans into me.

"I don't remember seeing biting as an option on my list." Looking up at me, her pupils are dilated.

"Remember you have the option to stop me at any time. What color are you?"

"Um, green for sure."

I escort her back to the office, stop and knock, waiting to enter until I hear a faint yes through the door. "I never know if Danielle is working or playing, so it's better to knock," I explain.

Danielle stands when we step inside.

"Which scene room on the south side is available?" Morgan's body briefly tenses. I don't speak or try to sway her decision. She'll have the final say.

Danielle checks the schedule. "The historical suite and a do-it-yourself room." She never changes her expression. None of us judge or care what happens here as long everyone is happy. My goal tonight is to help Morgan let go of her inhibitions while I give her a few of the best orgasms of her life.

"We'll take the do-it-yourself room."

Danielle taps a couple of keys on the computer and says, "It's yours. Enjoy."

I lead Morgan down the hall, stopping before we re-enter the club. "From this point on your gaze is down, don't speak unless I ask a question, and don't argue. Trust me. Can you do that?"

"Yes, Sir." Her words are soft, but I hear her clearly.

We walk straight through to the back of the building and past the renaissance room. I key in a code, open the door and walk inside. Morgan follows without taking a peek at the room. My dick has never been so hard at just the thought of doing a scene with a woman. Every twitch is painful, but I'm not going to hurry things tonight. "Undress, fold your clothes, and place them on the chair to your right."

The room gives the illusion of being private, but with one flick of my wrist, the curtains to the galley open and I see just how many people have filled the theater seating. They're sitting on the edge of their seats, like a group of eager med students observing their teacher perform the miracles knowledge has given us over the human body. I turn to gauge Morgan's reaction. Her eyes don't lift, but her hands freeze as the ties to her dress come undone and she clutches the fabric to her chest. Her breathing becomes rapid.

"Morgan, still green?" I ask from the opposite side of a padded table equipped with stirrups and restraints. She can't see the drawers full of toys in the cabinet behind her, but she knows they're there, along with the incredible collection of paddles and whips displayed on the wall.

Her answer is spoken too softly, I can't accept it. "Speak up, Morgan."

"Green, Sir," she says louder, but she doesn't move.

"Then drop your dress. Expose that beautiful body to me and everyone in the gallery." When I finally allow her to look, she won't be able to make out the faces just darkened shadows of the men and women who've congregated to observe.

Its obvious Danielle has been busy informing the members I'll be performing a scene; something I haven't done in over a year.

Morgan lets her dress fall to the floor, picks it up, then folds and places it on the seat of the chair. Her lush, round ass is a sight to behold. I want to touch it. Bite it. Brand it as mine. She unsnaps her thong, drops it to the clothing pile, and turns toward me.

I haven't been this wired since my first mission. That time in my life was a combination of excitement, nerves, determination, and, yeah, fear. Right now those nerves are screaming for me to bury myself deep inside her.

"Turn around and keep your eyes on me. In this room, it's just you and me."

"Yes, Sir." The slight tremor in her voice shows her strength and passion.

"Well done," I brag. "Now get on the table and lie back." Morgan complies but looks at me and lifts her eyebrows. "You may speak in here."

"Thank you, Sir." She climbs on the table and turns over. Her eyes are wide but she accepts the exposure of her body. Her trust almost undoes me.

Morgan's mouth is slightly open and her chest rises and falls like a sprinter at the end of a race. She's impossible to resist. I lean over and kiss her. My tongue sweeps past her lips and her back bows offering me her breasts. I release her mouth to tease her nipples with my tongue and fingers.

A strap is attached to the table and I place it across her ribs and secure it. Her eyes are wide but I don't see fear. I see her desire and I'm comfortable taking the next step. I walk to the storage drawer, open it, select two sets of lined leather cuffs, and stuff a blindfold in my pocket. Morgan is watching every move I make. "Put your arms by your side, bend your knees, and press your heels against your ass." Without a word or any effort, she follows my instructions. "You're doing great."

"Thank you, Sir."

"Spread your knees. Wider." I place a set of cuffs on the table on either side of her body and secure her wrist. After ensuring the restraint is not too tight, I buckle the second cuff around her ankle. Moving to the other side, I repeat the process and then walk to the foot of the table. She's spread wide open and my eyes feast on her pink flesh. Morgan in bondage is an image I'll never forget. "My God, you're beautiful."

"Thank you, Sir."

"Comfortable?"

"Yes, Sir." She lifts her head, trying to see how wide open I have spread her legs. She breathes out a long sigh.

"Color," I ask.

"Green, Sir. Very. I am completely under your control."

"That's the plan. You are breathtaking and your scent is making me insane." I peel back her outer lips and lean down with my face inches from her sweet pussy, breathing in her desire. "You smell amazing."

"Zack," she moans softly.

I'm dying to touch her so I slide my index finger around the inner edge of her pussy, not giving her exactly what she wants. She tries to lift her hips but the restraint I buckled across her body prevents much movement. "I can't wait any longer to taste you." I run my tongue from back to front, filling my mouth with her juices. I work her clit, pressing down, and squeezing her with my fingers.

"Oh, Zack. I need . . ."

If I continue touching her clit she'll come, so I pull away.

"You stopped. Come back," she moans.

"You will come only when I tell you to."

"Please."

I smack the inside of her thigh with my hand. "I make the decisions. Remember that."

"Yes, Sir," she snaps her words out whip-fast.

"Are you trying to get me to punish you?"

"No, Sir. I'm sorry, Sir."

"Color?"

"Still green." She's so beautiful, lying there, open and willing to let me do whatever I want to her. Her pussy glistens. I want another taste, but have one more step to do. Retrieving the blindfold from my pocket, I cover her eyes. Morgan's body tenses.

"Relax." I kiss my way from her cheek to her collar bone nipping her soft skin and licking away the pain. "This way you have to rely on your senses and won't anticipate what's going to happen next. "This will be a long night." I run my finger through her wet pussy, stroking back and forth before inserting my finger.

"So good," she moans.

I slide a second finger inside her and pump, curling into her G-spot, enjoying the lusty sounds she makes. "I fucking love how responsive your body is to me."

Removing my fingers, I move to her breasts. Wetting both nipples with her juices, I suck and lick that sweet flavor into my mouth. Morgan's bottom lip is between her teeth, and she's still trying to lift her chest for me.

I open one of the storage doors under the table and select a bottle of body lotion. It's time to take it up a notch.

****

Morgan

Zack's mouth pulls away from my breast with a pop. "Please don't stop." My nipples grow even harder as cool air rushes across my skin.

"Just slowing things down a little." Drops of liquid dot my foot and slowly continue up to my thighs. "How long since you had a good massage?"

"Forever. But . . ." My words trail off as strong hands spread a citrus-scented lotion on my right ankle and up my leg. He kneads my muscles with his hands, softly rubbing and squeezing. His hand moves closer to the apex of my thighs, which are spread wide open. "Your hands are one of my favorite parts of your body coming right after your mouth and dick."

Zack chuckles. "Well, thank you." He places a kiss right on the top of my pussy. Just a simple peck but it ratchets my need higher.

That Zack and everyone in that gallery can see my most private parts should be embarrassing, but, instead, I'm turned on in a way I've never been before and I hope his attention to my legs also includes manipulations of my weeping pussy. I groan out my frustration when he stops and moves to my other leg. A whine escapes my lips.

"Relax." His voice is raspier than usual and sounds needy. "Breathe and enjoy being the center of attention."

I can't hold back my smile. "That's hard to do when you stop before reaching the part of me that's dying to be massaged."

Zack chuckles. "And what part would that be?" He's driving me to the point of pleading.

"My pussy," I beg. "Please, Sir, my pussy." The amount of fluid that's coating and drenching my thighs will soon puddle on the table.

"It's my pussy," he reminds me. "And it's rosy, pink, and so damn beautiful. Mine."

His warm breath washes over my wet flesh, pulling a groan from deep inside me. I try to lift my hips to get closer to his mouth but the strap across my ribs and the cuffs restrict my movements.

Zack's fingers open me and his tongue strokes me and hovers over my clit. "Do not come. If you do without permission, I will punish your sweet ass."

I cry out when he gives my pussy an open mouth kiss and then works his tongue in and out of me. An impending climax boils up, and I try to fight it back. Suddenly, there's nothing but cool air on my burning flesh. "Wait." A few seconds later, I add, "Sir."

"You were close to losing control." Zack kisses my belly button and continues the massage.

"You're killing me." Edging, that's what he's doing. I read about it on the internet. It's repeated denial of an orgasm so when you do come it will be much more powerful. So far my body isn't buying into that theory. I clamp my mouth shut and try to leave the decision making to him. A heavy sigh escapes when Zack's hands slip under my breasts, lifting them into his palms. One pinch of my nipples and I'm racing down the orgasm highway at full speed.

"Color?"

"If green is still go, emerald."

Zack chuckles. His mouth covers mine in a crushing kiss. I open for him and our tongues merge, conveying the passion we're both feeling. His mouth moves to my ear. "My impatient beauty. How am I ever going to train you to be submissive?"

I want to see his face badly. His eyes will tell me if he's displeased or teasing. "Please don't give up trying."

"Never. You're a natural-born sub. The most receptive woman I've ever had."

"You can have me right now," I respond quickly, hoping to encourage him. My pussy spasms and additional moisture flows from me. God, I've never needed to come so badly.

"I know." He pulls my bottom lip into his mouth and nips it with his teeth. "You're all mine."

"I need you inside me."

"Maybe later, after I've finished your massage." He kisses me again, it's a long, lingering soft touch. "For now, I'm enjoying touching your body." Zack pats my leg. Hang on."

I hear the slide of a drawer opening and closing. Then a soft cloth rubs my limbs and torso wiping off excess lotion. My skin warms under the long strokes. Shit. Something cold rubs across my outer lips, separating them. I gasp when the vibrations start. It slides back and forth through my folds and then slips inside me. Every synapse in my brain fires. "Ohmygodohmygod."

Zack sucks my clit while the vibrations grow stronger. I feel as I'm levitating off the table. "Zack, I can't stop it." I'm babbling. My body has taken over and there's no slowing down.

"Come for me. Now."

My world shatters into a million shiny pieces, shards fly behind my eyes like a huge broken mirror. My mind is in a place I've never been to. It's as if I've been lifted into the clouds and am floating freely among them.

My next recognition is hearing Zack whispering to me. The blindfold is gone and he's holding me in his arms. I open my eyes and melt into his dark eyes.

"Hello." The expression on his face isn't one I've seen before, but I want to see it every day for the rest of my life. Passion, pride, and gentleness radiate from him. "I've been waiting for you." Zack strokes the loose hair that escaped my ponytail away from my face and presses his lips against my forehead.

"What happened? Where are we? The last thing I remember was a feeling of weightless ecstasy. Tell me I didn't fall asleep."

"You're in a quiet space where I can hold you until you're fully awake and aware of your surroundings. You didn't sleep, it's called subspace and brought on by an influx of adrenaline and endorphins. You went past experiencing your orgasm to a place in your mind of pure bliss."

"What about you? I just had the orgasm of my life and gave you nothing."

"Sure you did. When you entered subspace, I experienced a deeper connection with you. You trusting that I can give you extreme pleasure is the greatest gift you can give me." Looking down at me, he cuddles me closer. His expression is incredibly serene and beautiful. "I've never felt a high such as the one I'm on right now. I should be thanking you."

I snuggle deeper into his warm chest. The feeling of being loved and protected fills my heart. No. Not loved. It's too soon for that; Zack and I have just started this relationship. Whatever I'm feeling right now is the after-effects of my orgasm. I close my eyes and listen to the rhythm of his heartbeat. I feel as if I've discovered my true self. "Zack."

"Hmm? What do you need?"

"More."

"You liked the vibrator?"

"I did, but I meant more of you."

Chapter 7

Zack

Morgan wants more of me. That bit of news pleases me. I want a hell of a lot more of her. She's a beautiful flower awakening in a brand new world full of excitement, sex, and emotions. Her soft whispers wrap around my heart, finding a home in places I've sworn to never allow another human to enter. I've purposely taken it easy on her, hoping not to scare her away. She's so fucking receptive to anything I give her, I want to throw her over my shoulder, carry her back to the room and fuck her until she can't walk without my help.

She moves in my arms, wiggling her ass over my very impatient dick. Leaning back, she smiles up at me. "I'm back."

"So you are." I lean down and taste her sweet lips. "Would you like to get dressed? You don't have to, we can sit right here until you're ready."

"What?" She lifts the blanket I have cocooned her in and looks under it.

I laugh at her wide eyes. She's not beyond being shocked. Not yet.

"I've been sleeping here naked all this time?"

"Yep. I took off the cuffs and blindfold and wrapped you tightly. Baby, no one gets to see your glorious tits or that delectable pussy of yours unless I want them to."

She laughs and I join her. "What if I'm a one and done type person?"

"Then the people in the gallery who got to witness that one-time show were fucking lucky." I stand, still holding her in my arms and carry her back to our room. Closing the door, I put her down and make sure she's steady on her feet.

Morgan slips her thong up her legs. "You didn't get to use the snaps." She demonstrates the easy off twin snaps.

I groan loudly. I'd finally gotten control of my dick but it springs to life with her demonstration. Morgan wearing a thong and her perky tits is almost too much. "I need to buy you a dozen more."

She wiggles into that dress that hugs her body, and I stare. She's so damn sexy she takes my breath away. I fucking can't get enough of her.

I hold back the groan building in my chest. I want to see this woman in every style of lingerie ever made.

Morgan turns her back to me and I snap the two small pieces of cloth at the back of her neck together. "I should have thanked you for the outfits earlier. That you stopped by and selected them for me makes me proud to wear them."

"Andrea talks too much." I turn Morgan to face me. "I'm guessing she also told you, I've never actually shopped for a woman."

"Yes, she did. I'm incredibly flattered." She takes down her hair, runs her fingers through it a few times, and secures it back into the high ponytail. "You have impeccable taste."

"In women for sure." I tug her against my chest. "Tonight we expanded your sexual boundaries and we're just getting started. Where have you been all my life? Never mind. You're here and we're going to make up for the lost time."

"Truth or lie?" Morgan's crystal blue eyes have a seriousness I haven't seen before.

"Truth." I've never been more truthful. "I'm not going anywhere." She melts into me and my mouth covers hers, our tongues giving and taking of each other.

"Me either." She slips on her shoes from hell and takes my hand. "I'm ready."

"Let me buy you another drink." I wrap my arm around her waist and lead her to the front of the club. A few members smile and nod as we pass. "They're acknowledging your bravery."

Danielle is leaning against the bar. She pushes off and walks to meet us. "Another Glendalough, boss?"

"Absolutely, and a glass of red for Morgan." Danielle walks around behind the bar and relays our order to the bartender, Van. He leans his elbows on the counter and smiles at Morgan. "I'll pour yours myself."

Morgan returns his smile and then turns to face me. "He's a big flirt."

"Come here." I tug her ponytail, running the silky strands through my fingers. I lead her to a couch close to the bar. "Yes. The ladies love Van. I also think he's offering, in a not so subtle way, to be our third."

Her back straightens. "You share women?"

"Never long term. Nick and I double-teamed a time or two when we were in the military. But I've never had a polyamorous relationship, and neither have Nick or Slider since I've known them. Occasionally, a dom who likes to watch his sub scene with another man or a member couple will want a third person to join them and one of us will help out."

"Help out?" Morgan glances around as if this is the first time she been here.

I take her hands in mine. "My participation in those scenes ended the night you walked into Gloss."

"Oh." Her gaze comes back to meet mine. "Good."

I can't help but smile. "Wait until you meet Slider. It's not uncommon for him to join a scene or invite a second male to join him and a sub in one of the open scene rooms where people can touch. He's the lover of the group."

"Slider can't possibly be the lover of you three." Morgan's lips curve up in a sexy grin. "I'm sure you hold that title." She thanks Danielle when the drinks arrive.

"I'm glad you think so." I'm also glad she's relaxed again.

"I have a question." Morgan's cheeks turn a soft shade of pink.

"Ask away."

"Was that edging you were doing to me? Not allowing me to come?"

I can't help but smile at her. She's been researching the lifestyle. It didn't appear to make her uncomfortable to ask. "Yes and no. Tonight wasn't near as intense as it can get, and we'll explore the benefits of denial again soon."

Morgan rolls her eyes. "That might kill me."

"I won't take it that far; I prefer your hot body alive and well." Morgan glances behind me and her smile vanishes. I turn to see Danielle carrying a folder and walking toward us.

Morgan turns away and sips her wine. "She's very beautiful. Have you two—?"

"No."

"Not even in a scene?"

I lean close to Morgan. "Never. Danielle may be curious about us since you're the first woman I've brought to the club."

"I can't tell you how much I like hearing that."

Danielle hands me the folder. "The information on Dale Loften and a couple of pages for you to sign."

"Thank you." I extend my hand to Morgan and help her stand. "Let's go into my office where we won't be interrupted."

Morgan steps into my workspace and looks around. Her gaze comes back to me when she stops at the oversized couch that runs along one wall. My mahogany desk and high-back leather chair take up one corner. My workspace is positioned so I can see the bank of monitors on the far wall. I open the folder, put it on my desk, and sit to read it. "I don't normally get this deep into people's background information, but this is different. Anyone who fucks with you will regret it."

Morgan walks to my bookcase and studies the only picture in my office. "And nobody gets to fuck with me but you."

I laugh at her smart crack. "You're right about that."

I glance over the findings, reading it silently. Loften is Criminal Court Justice Steven Loften's son. That family has quite a pedigree plus they're drowning in money. It doesn't surprise me Loften doesn't think rules apply to him. I remember the news story where the good judge awarded sixty days community service to a couple of college boys who'd been charged with assault and rape. The public and the news had cried injustice, but the story slowly faded away with no repercussions for the judge.

"I never met his family or any of his friends," Morgan says holding the picture of my family. "You were a cute kid."

"It's my only memory of my mom and dad smiling at the same time."

She returns the picture and walks over to me. "I remember Dale complaining he'd never been able to please his dad."

"I know what it's like to have a father who's disappointed in his son. Didn't turn me into an asshole. It taught me not to take shit off anyone." I clamp my mouth shut. Sharing that was unexpected and unnecessary.

"You most certainly are not an asshole." Morgan cups my cheek and rubs my jawline with her thumb. "I like you with a little stubble."

"I can be convinced to leave a little when I shave. Whisker burns on the inside of your thighs will mark you as mine. Remind you of me even when we're not together."

Morgan sits in the chair next to me. I close the file and turn my attention to her.

"You've taught me so much. I don't feel vanilla anymore."

"Bullshit," I say with a smile. "You're about as vanilla as I am." Morgan is beaming at me and I meet her smile with one of my own. "You could be the poster girl for sensuous. You're beautiful, very responsive, exciting, experimental, sexy as sin, and very capable of asking for what you want."

Describing her took no thinking on my part; the words just flew out of my mouth, and I meant every one of them.

I pull her off her chair and onto my lap. "Want more proof you're not vanilla?"

"From you? Always." Morgan lifts her short skirt higher and swings her legs around to straddle me.

It takes a mere flick of my fingers and the breakaway thong is in two pieces. "God, I fucking love these. Next time, I'm going with you and you'll try on every piece of lingerie Andrea has to offer."

Morgan laughs as she lifts her hips and I push the thong to the floor. She leans forward and kisses my cheek. "I fucking love your dimple."

"Listen to your dirty mouth. I do hope I've corrupted you."

She pulls the corner of her bottom lip into her mouth. "If I'm corrupted, it's in the very best way."

I slip my hand between us and cup her smooth pussy. "Mine."

"Yours."

I dip two fingers inside her. "You are so responsive."

"I want you." Her lips find mine. This kiss isn't demanding or frantic. It's Morgan continuing to blossom and learn.

In an unusual move for me, I tilt my head back and give her control. "Take what you need."

Her tongue explores the inside of my mouth, tasting, and stroking. "I need you inside me."

She doesn't have to say it twice. I grab a condom from a desk drawer, lift her high enough to unzip my slacks and cover my dick. "I'm all yours."

"Damn right you are." She takes me in her hand and lines me up at her entrance. Slowly sinking onto me, she stops when she's pressed against my pubic bone. Savoring the sensations, neither of us moves for a few moments. Morgan leans down and rests her forehead against mine. The connection between us swamps me and the word forever keeps running through my head.

After my divorce, I decided I didn't ever want or need a committed relationship again. Now, I realize just how wrong I was.

Morgan sits up straight and rocks her hips forward. "Hmm. You feel so good inside me. I can't wait for our tests and the results to come back."

"Me either."

We lock gazes, neither of us looking away. Barely moving, she rubs her clit against me. A tender smile lights up her face. Jesus, she looks almost angelic. Her breasts fit perfectly in my hands and I stroke my thumbs gently back and forth over her nipples.

"You're holding the reins," I whisper. I've never allowed topping from the bottom. Yet, somehow, I understand Morgan needs this, and I want to give it, no, need to give it to her. If I have to count backward in threes, I will not come until she does.

Her movements are slow as she continues to grind herself against me. I swear my dick grows harder and larger than it has ever been. Morgan's expression is the most erotic thing I've ever seen. Her hips increase their movement, slowly picking up speed. She pulls upward and then slams down hard.

"Ride me. Take what you need."

The next few minutes are frenzied as we both race toward our orgasms. Her hands clasp my shoulders tightly, nails dig into my skin, and her eyes close. "Please," she whispers. "I need you to take control."

"Fuck, yes." I slide my hands under her ass, lift, and pound into her, giving her every inch of me again and again.

"Close. I'm so close. Harder," she pleads.

I fucked her harder and rougher with each thrust until her pussy clenches me, squeezing and pulsing.

"Come now. Cover me with your juices."

"Yes. Oh. Yes." Her nails dig into my chest as we crest together. Her moans and mine blend as cum surges from me again and again. I can't wait to put my condoms away and feel her hot pussy when I come. Sweat is running down our faces when her head falls to my chest. "That was . . ."

"It certainly was." Chests heaving, neither of us moves for the next few minutes. Our orgasms have sent us both into a place of calm and peace.

"Can we just stay like this forever?" Morgan lifts her head and smiles.

"Sure. The only problem I see is when Danielle wanders in to close up for the night." I reach under her, not wanting to pull out of her but careful to hold the condom in place. "I'm in no hurry."

She points at a closed door in the far corner. "Is that a bathroom?"

"Yes. Complete with a shower and all the toiletries you could possibly need."

"I'll be back." She lifts off me with a sigh. "I feel the loss of you already."

"Me, too. Sex with you takes the act to a whole new level."

"Truth or lie?"

"The most truthful thing I've ever said."

Morgan searches my face, and I let her see the honesty in my statement. She smiles, a little bit coy and a whole lot proud, as if, for the first time, she believes she truly is a sex goddess in my arms. She stands and retrieves the two-piece thong from the floor then disappears behind the closed door. By the time she returns, she's repaired the damage to her hairstyle, is dressed and looks like she'd just stepped out of my dreams.

"Let's get out of here." I offer her my arm. The touch of her small hand gives me a strange sense of pride.

"Let's go." She nods and smiles.

I stop near the dance floor where Danielle is watching as the couples are moving in slow motion.

"I left the Loften file on my desk and signed the applications. He'll never set foot in here again. I'll have our PI keep tabs on him for a couple of days. I don't intend to take any shit off him."

"Will you be here tomorrow?" Danielle asks.

"Yes, you can take the day off." It's the right thing to do. Danielle works a lot of hours at Silken. It means I'll have to be here for the make-ready team. That alone takes up a few hours as each play area is cleaned and restocked. Either Danielle, Gabriel, or I are always here to ensure Silken is spotless before we open. It will prevent me from spending all day Sunday with Morgan unless she wants to hang out with me while I log in deliveries and work on leftover paperwork.

Nick walks in the door, meeting us on the way out. It's late and not unusual for him or Slider to stop by after closing their clubs. "You two leaving already?"

"Yes. How was the crowd at Gloss tonight?"

"Packed again. We reached the maximum number of people allowed, with a line waiting outside."

"Good. Keeping them wanting is a good policy." I wink at Morgan, smiling at the flush still on her cheeks. I turn her away from my partner and say, "Later."

"Don't forget we're having a football party at Gloss tomorrow. It starts at seven."

"I can't make it. I've given Danielle the day off and will be here all afternoon for deliveries. I'll have just enough time to go home and clean up before coming back to open the club."

"Hey, Morgan, if you're tired of this guy, you're invited. But fair warning: don't show up wearing any jersey without a Bears' logo on the front." Nick's eyebrows lift. "It's always a wild party."

"What?" She clamps her hand on her chest. "The only jersey in my closet is blue with a silver star on a helmet."

"No! You'll start a riot." Nick laughs, watching me closely. I growl at him, mostly because he expects it.

"Good night, Nick. We'll talk soon." I stop to tell Gabriel I'm driving Morgan home, explaining to her my car was in the parking lot and her face brightens.

"You were already here at work and stopped to ride in with Gabriel to pick me up?"

"I did. He was ready to leave when I decided my paperwork could wait. I wanted to see you."

Morgan slips her hand in mine. "I like that. A lot."

We walk to my car and I help her get seated. I fasten her seatbelt and kiss her before I close her door. I walk around to the driver's side and slide in. "I didn't mean I'm taking you to your apartment. By home, I meant I am taking you to mine."

Morgan shakes her head. "I'd like that, but I really shouldn't. My friends will be out looking for me if I'm not home tomorrow when they come looking for a full report on tonight."

I know she's experienced a lot of new things in the past couple of days and probably needs some time away from me to digest everything she's experienced in our short time together. I'm hooked and have been since we first met but I'll give her the breathing room she needs. I reach over and rest my hand on her knee. "I'll take you to your apartment on one condition."

"What's that?" I can see the renewed excitement in her eyes. She wants what I'm offering.

"I want to see where this takes us. I don't want to put an end date on what we have."

Morgan's gaze holds mine for a second. I can see in an instant she agrees with me. She leans across the console and runs her fingers across my cheek. "I don't know how you do it. Two jobs would kill me, yet you still have the most incredible sex drive. I want to continue exploring mine with you."

I bring her hand to my lips and kiss her palm gently. "Being the boss is convenient. My staff is incredibly self-sufficient, so I don't have to be in the office unless I have meetings. But this is a busy week coming up, and I won't have a lot of spare time. A couple of my largest investors have their account reviews scheduled. After tomorrow, I'll be too busy to sleep late in the morning."

"You're lucky to have people you trust."

"You're right. Earning my trust isn't an easy thing."

"You were very much in love with your ex-wife and she broke your trust."

In the past, I've refused to discuss my divorce with anyone, but Morgan's voice is sincere and compassionate. "I thought so at the time. Hell, it may have been my fault. I worked day and night building the brokerage firm. I left her alone a lot."

"My grandmother believed a person shouldn't let other people's failures influence their attitude. I forgive them and move on."

"Really? Even Dale Loften?"

"I don't hate him. I've cut him out of my life."

"So you don't hold a grudge of any kind?"

"I try not to. Of course, sometimes I fail." Morgan chuckles.

"What's funny?"

"You're pretty slick. That's twice you've turned the subject around and avoided talking about yourself."

"It's a talent." I squeeze her knee just as she yawns behind her hand.

"Sorry." She shuffles in her seat.

"You've had a busy night. We're about twenty minutes from your apartment. Close your eyes. You're safe with me."

She slips off those shoes that hurt her feet, leans the seat back a notch, and closes her eyes. "Zack."

"Hmm?"

"I know I'm safe with you."

My gut clenches at Morgan's words. Glancing over, it strikes me how beautiful she is at rest. Her eyes are closed and her body's relaxed. I fish around in my head for an explanation of why I'm so attracted to her. We're moving fast, yet I don't want to slow down. Shaking my head, I keep my eyes on the road.

The second I turn off the ignition, Morgan opens her eyes and glances at the clock on the dash of my car. "It's still early. Want a cup of coffee?"

I laugh at her eagerness. "Absolutely not. You know what will happen if we get close to a bed. I need you to be strong and send me away."

Chapter 8

Morgan

I stretch my muscles and rollover toward the clock. I pull my phone from under the pillow, open my eyes, and check my texts. The FaceTime calls and texts Zack and I have exchanged the past week have been romantic and hot, but I miss his physical presence. That's not all of him I miss, but I'm hoping we'll end this physical drought soon. My cell beeps and I hope it's not Dale again. His interest in me has been unrelenting since the incident at the club. I refuse to answer his calls, so he's resorted to texting. I've received one every day this week begging me to give him another chance. Each one has gotten nastier until I threatened to register a complaint with the police.

This text makes me smile.

Zack: *Two more days.*

Morgan: *Two more days until what?*

Zack: *So that's the way it's going to be? Then I guess you'll have to wait and see.*

Morgan: *I can't wait. I want you.*

Zack: *I'm dying. Send me a pic of your perfect breasts.*

I've never done anything as outrageous as taking a nude picture of any part of my body and sharing it. Yet here I am sending a second naked photograph to Zack. I pull off my tank top and pinch my nipples into stiff peaks. Then snap a selfie and then hit send.

Zack: *Your nipples are begging for my teeth.*

Morgan: *They only get this hard for you.*

Zack: *Fuck. I have a raging hard-on and a client is due soon.*

He's killing me. I can't think of him without soaking my panties. I head to the bathroom and take a quick shower. I dry off, pick up my hairdryer, and then hear someone knocking. I wrap a towel around me and run to the door. Through the peephole I see the UPS driver walking away. I open the door far enough to grab the box and carry it inside. It's addressed to me from a company I've never ordered from. Taking time to open it will put me in heavy morning traffic, but I can't wait. I grab a kitchen knife, drop the box on my bed, and slice open the tape.

Inside, wrapped in white tissue paper, are small stacks of breakaway thongs. I laugh while I count five different colors. I slide on a purple pair, snap a picture, and send it to Zack. I hurry through getting ready for work and sprint to my car. I've never driven so fast, but I somehow make it to work on time. I slide into my chair and check my boss's calendar and appointments. Then I take a peek at my cell for a text. I'm not too disappointed since I know Zack's with a client, but I turn the sound down and leave my phone on my desk.

"Good morning." I look up and Chels is holding a small, white sack in front of me that smells like heaven. "Cinnamon roll?"

"Thank you. I didn't have time to grab breakfast." Breathing in the sweet aroma, I reach for the sack and she moves it out of reach, "Gimmee," I whine.

"Not until I know what caused the smile on your face . . . no, the smirk, on your face."

I crook my finger for her to come closer so I can whisper. Nobody in this office needs to know about my gifts from Zack. "You remember I said Zack loved the breakaway panties and was going to buy me a dozen?"

"He didn't?" Her smile widens.

"A dozen of five different colors."

"Really? No shit?" Chels laughs and it vibrates down the hall. "God, I love this guy."

"I sent him a picture."

"He's probably hard and horny just looking at it."

"I hope so." I realize my comment was sincere.

Chels is still laughing when she hands me the bag. "We'll talk more at lunch."

My morning is full as I lay out my boss's travel for the following week. I field his calls and type up a few letters for him while forcing myself not to check my cell every few minutes.

I've grown used to hearing Zack's voice at night when I'm at home alone in bed. I've discovered phone sex can be exciting and rewarding. Even though we've only known each other for a short time, he's changed my life and I can't wait to see him. Because of him, I'm learning to be proud of myself and not to be afraid to ask for what I want. My body yearns for him; he's become very important to me. The video phone sex we've had is great but it's not enough.

"Are you okay?" My boss is peering at me over his glasses.

"Yes, I'm fine." I can't allow my mind to drift like that at work. "Did you need something?"

"I'm having lunch with my wife so I may be longer than usual."

"Enjoy." I hope I managed to sound professional, but long lunches have taken on a new meaning for me. I yearn for the day I can take them with Zack. I text Chels to meet me at the elevator in ten minutes. I shut down my computer and grab my cell.

Chels is holding the elevator door open when I get there. "Kayla is meeting us outside. We need our daily update on your multimillionaire lover."

I push the button for the ground floor. "I know nothing about Zack being a millionaire. I assume he's financially secure, but he doesn't talk about it."

"Really? If you'd Googled his net worth you'd know."

I lift my eyebrows. "You didn't?"

"Of course I didn't." Chels rolls her eyes. "Kayla did."

I love Chels's sense of humor but I'm not interested in learning about Zack's money. "I don't care if he's rich or not. He makes me happy. End of story."

"It's no secret you're happy. The smile on your face has every woman in the office asking me if you have a new man."

"The rumor mill must be working overtime. What did you tell them?"

"To ask you."

We step out of the elevator, and I elbow her arm. "Seriously?"

"If those nosey bitches want to know, they should have the guts to talk to you."

I loop my arm through hers and we turn the corner laughing. We join Kayla, who's waiting outside on the sidewalk.

"Zaszo's Sub Shop is closest," Kayla suggests. "I'm starving." She's already walking in that direction.

"Fine with me." I fall in step next to her and she tosses her arm over my shoulder. "No more checking into Zack's net worth, past life, or present. Okay?"

"At all?" Kayla's hurt expression is so fake, I laugh.

"At all." I try to sound serious, but when the three of us are together that's hard to do.

The sub shop is busy and we're stuck standing in line to place our orders and get our drinks before we take the last empty table. We're talking about work when Kayla looks over my shoulder and her eyes widen. A hand touches my shoulder.

"May I join you, ladies?" Zack's voice sends shivers down my body. I stand and turn into his arms. The twinkle in his eyes and the satisfied smile on his face steals my breath away.

"Anytime." I give him a quick kiss and he takes the empty chair next to me. "How did you know where to find us?"

"Gabriel had just dropped me off in front of your building when I saw you heading this way. So I followed."

"I'm glad you did. I don't believe I've formally introduced you to my friends. Chelsea Coffman, Kayla Britton, meet Zack Pierce."

"It's nice to meet you both." Zack stands and shakes their hands just as our lunch arrives. "I think I'll grab a sandwich. Be right back." He takes a couple of steps and turns back to us. "Can I get you, ladies, anything?"

"We're good," I answer because Chels and Kayla are busy staring at Zack.

Kayla wipes her mouth with the back of her hand. "He's even more gorgeous close-up. Why can't I find a guy who's a gentleman, rich, and fucks me silly?

"He cooks too." I couldn't resist adding that fact.

Kayla lets out a low moan. "When are you taking us to one of his clubs?"

"Are you interested in going?"

"Hell, yes," Kayla answers.

"That's not my decision to make, but I can ask."

I hear a buzzing sound and realize I left my phone on silent. Zack returns just as I reach for my purse and he helps me unhook it from my chair. I dig my phone out of the mess of receipts and makeup jumbled inside my bag and look at the caller ID. I frown and glance up at Chels and Kayla. "It's our apartment manager."

"Mr. Pritchard, is everything okay?" I catch every other excited word he utters but it's obvious something is very wrong. My chair squeaks its protest as I shove it back and stand. "Of course, Mr. Pritchard. I'm on my way." My gut's in turmoil, rolling around in confusion and my hands tremble when I end the call.

"What's wrong?" Zack's hand rests on my shoulder.

"My apartment has been vandalized."

"Gabriel's right outside." Zack pulls his cell phone from his pocket.

"Chels, will you explain my absence—" I don't finish before she's nodding.

"Go. I'll take care of it. Kayla and I will be there as soon as we can."

Gabriel is already at the curb when we walk outside. He hops out and opens the door to the SUV and Zack helps me in before sitting next to me. Gabriel quickly slides behind the wheel and asks, "Where to?"

"Morgan's apartment has been vandalized. We're going to need a cleanup crew on standby."

"On it." Gabriel pulls his phone to his ear and speaks softly.

Zack covers my hand with his. "The police will probably want you to go inside and determine what, if anything, is missing. We won't know if they'll collect fingerprints until we speak with them."

"I hope there's not a lot of damage."

"We'll figure this out." His voice is calm and reassuring, but I can see a muscle in his jaw twitch. "Can you think of anyone who'd do this?"

I feel as if a steel band has wrapped around my chest. I feel guilty for not telling Zack about Dale. "I should've told you about the phone calls and texts I received from Dale this past week. I thought he'd go away if I ignored him. How could I have been so stupid?"

Eyes dark as midnight look into mine. "You are not stupid. Now tell me what you're talking about."

I want Zack to kiss me. Hold me. Never let me go. I've never had anyone but my Nana to protect me until now. Tears seep into my eyes but I blink them away and tell Zack how the messages and texts from Dale had gotten more and more threatening.

"Yes, you should've told me after the first text. You're important to me and I won't tolerate anyone fucking with you." Zack unhooks his seat belt, slides over and wraps his arms around me. He takes out his phone and calls somebody. "Jackson, find out where and how Dale Loften spent the last three days." Zack ends the call and answers my unasked question. "My private investigator will get answers. Maybe someone at the apartment complex saw what happened."

"I can't thank you enough. Having you in my life is like walking out of a fog into the sunshine." I take a deep breath and my lungs fill with Zack's scent. This is a side of Zack I've never seen. It frightens me a little, but, at the same time, I'm overwhelmed and touched.

"We'll gather some of your things and you'll stay with me until this is sorted out."

Before I can reply, Gabriel parks at my apartment building. Zack and I hurry up the stairs where my apartment manager meets us. and excitedly explains the damage. He calms Mr. Pritchard down and we move on to speak with the police officer on site. Zack introduces me, hands him a card, and I share my information with him. After answering questions, we're going to be allowed inside with instructions not to touch anything and to make a list of anything missing. He stops and says something I can't hear, and Mr. Pritchard smiles at me before leaving.

"What did you say to him?"

A slow smile creeps up Zack's cheeks. "I assured him that he could get on with his daily business. Let's take a look."

My nerves have me about to jump out of my skin but when Zack takes my hand, I know everything will be okay. Painted on the outside of the front door is the word SLUT. I hear Zack growl as he leans down and studies the busted door. "You don't engage the deadbolt when you leave?"

"No, but I always use it when I'm home." I wait for a comment but he just nods his head.

He pushes the door open and leads me into the living room. Books, lamps, and what few pictures I have are strewn across the floor, all of it damaged when the furniture was upended. I don't realize tears are running down my cheeks until Zack turns me to face him and tenderly thumbs my cheeks dry.

"It's nothing we can't fix," Zack's words reassure me, but I can see some things are beyond repair. "Let's check out the rest."

With each step I take, the more I want to wrap my fingers around Dale's neck and squeeze. I've never experienced this feeling of being violated.

I don't own anything of great value, but it's mine, bought with my hard-earned money. I kneel and pick up the broken frame that holds a picture of my mom and dad. "Nana had a few pieces of jewelry that don't hold any real value. I kept them because they were hers."

"Let's check on those first." Zack and I walk upstairs to my bedroom.

I hold my breath as I open the top drawer on the chest next to my bed. The jewelry box is upended, as I expected, and I immediately shuffle through, retrieving all the pieces that Nana had left me. "Everything's here." I hold two pairs of earrings and one ring out to Zack. "Will you put these in your pocket?"

"Yes. They'll be safe with me."

I nod and he slips them into his suit coat pocket and then I turn to continue surveying the damage. It's a small but perfect bedroom. I added a room-size rug to cover the carpet and splurged on plum, five-hundred-count sheets with a matching plush comforter. The drawers on my dresser are pulled out and dumped on the floor. The closet door is open and small pieces of blue spandex are scattered across the floor. It's the dress I wore to Club Silken. I turn toward the bed where I left the box of my new thongs. It's gone. I rip the comforter off the bed and start flinging the already tossed clothes in the air, looking for Zack's gift.

"Hey." He crosses the room in three strides and pulls me into his arms. I bury my head in his chest as fresh, angry tears soak his shirt. I tremble with a need to do something, anything. But what?

"Together, we'll make this right. I promise it'll be okay."

"No, it won't." I've reached the ugly cry level and can't stop.

Zack steps back and says, "Talk to me."

"My thongs." I hiccup. "They're gone."

"The only thing missing is your panties?"

I shrug. "Who knows what else, but the thongs you bought and had delivered this morning are gone. That bastard took them," I snap at Zack.

Zack's face splits into a wide grin and a chuckle rolls from his chest. "Did he take the pair you wore Saturday night?"

I walk into the bathroom and open the hamper that holds the laundry I've put off all week. "No. My dirty clothes are untouched. So what?"

"Stupid bastard. I would've taken those for sure."

"Gross."

"Not at all." Zack pulls me into his arms. Because of the man with his arms around me, my anger is gone in a flash. He grounds me like no other. "They still smelled like you."

"That's sick," I whisper, looking up into his eyes. I do my best not to smile.

"Makes sense to me." He places his hand on my ass. "Are you wearing a pair now?"

"Maybe?" The warm brown that is so sexy has replaced the deeper flecks of anger in his eyes.

"Let's see what the police want to do since this isn't a random crime. Then my crew can get in here and clean things up before securing your apartment for the night." His hand moves to my back, rubbing circles. "You're staying with me, and I won't take no for an answer."

"Zack—"

Before I can argue he says, "I like the idea of you staying at my house."

"You do?"

"With or, preferably, without a breakaway thong, and since my blood test came back clean, no more barriers between us because of me."

"That's why you came to have lunch with me?"

"I wanted to give you this." Zack hands me a sealed envelope, kisses my forehead, and leans back in his chair.

I run a finger through the seal, open it, and read with a smile. I want to tease him but can't keep my face straight. "Not because of me either."

"There's nothing that feels better, and I can't wait."

My shoulders relax. Regardless of what my apartment looks like, I'll sleep in Zack's arms tonight.

Chapter 9

Morgan

It's been almost two months since I moved into Zack's penthouse. I still have my apartment, but with every passing day, more of my stuff gets stashed in his closet, his drawers, and his bathroom. He's proven to be right about having the blood tests. Sex without a condom, feeling his skin against my skin, filling me with his cum, is wonderful.

Zack hands me a steaming mug of coffee. "You don't mind brunch for lunch, do you?"

"Considering its almost noon and I'm starving, anything sounds wonderful." I add cream, lean against the counter, and stir, hoping to cool it down enough to drink quickly.

The look in his dark eyes excites me. "Sleeping late is a luxury for me, but you wore me out last night."

"Let's agree we wore each other out." Truth is, I crave his touch, his mouth, and his body. I've never known a man whose dark gaze could cause me to overheat and forget all my inhibitions at warp speed.

He moves around his kitchen with ease. The white cabinets, pale grey walls, and slate appliances fit his personality. They're smart, tasteful, and beautiful. I doubt he'd like them to be called beautiful, but it's the truth.

"Happy two-month anniversary." Zack sets a plate full of muffins on the counter in front of me. "Mrs. Owens made banana nut just for you."

"She spoils me." I take a bite of the muffin and wash it down with a sip of coffee. "That's delicious."

"She likes you." He brings his coffee to the table and sits. "Bring your coffee and muffins."

"That's true," I agree, sitting across from him.

"I like you too." He pulls a small, flat box from his pants pockets and places it next to the plate of muffins. I look at him and melt at the wide smile on his face. "Open it."

"Thank you." How he turns me into a puddle of emotions is amazing.

He chuckles. "You don't know what it is yet."

"I'll love it regardless." I gently remove the lid, pull the soft velvet out of the way, and find a stunning pair of graduated drop diamond earrings. They're the style that makes your neck look long and sexy. I stand, squeeze myself between his body and the table to sit on his lap, peppering his face with kisses. "They're beautiful." I hurry to the bathroom, put them on, and pull my hair back behind my ears. I use my fake model walk when I return to the kitchen. This time I sit astride him. "You shouldn't have. They're too expensive."

He gives me a cute smirk. "Not your decision to make. I'm glad you like them."

"I love them." I bite my tongue, keeping how I feel for him inside.

Zack's been super busy at work and knows my apartment has been ready for over a month, but he hasn't brought up me going back home, and, by this point, he's etched a permanent place in my heart. I'm sure that's not what he wants, and I take a deep breath and broach the subject.

"Listen, Zack, it isn't fair that I'm living here for free while you pay for everything. Maybe, it's time for me to go home." I feel his body go rigid as the muscles in his thighs tighten under me.

"Is that what you want?" His gaze bores into me.

"I'm not trying to push you into anything," I say honestly. He stands, placing my feet on the floor, and then steps back away from me.

"You're not. I happen to like waking up in the morning with your legs tangled around mine."

My brain is whirling. I know he's not talking about love, but I'm so close, if not already there. Regardless of whether I stay or not, I'm going to be hurt. Part of me screams *run* and the other part of me wants to stay as long as he'll have me.

"Keep your apartment if it makes you feel secure. I don't want to take away your independence and I understand how important your friends are to you." He moves next to my chair, pulls me to my feet, and touches his forehead to mine. "Stay. Please."

"Yes, Sir." His lips cover mine. They're warm and soft, and the kiss is tender. I stay in his arms, leaning my face against his chest, hoping my heart will survive when he's ready to move on.

"I'm glad that's settled. Let's finish breakfast." His smile lightens my mood and I refuse to linger on what might happen tomorrow. I push the negative thoughts away.

We fall into easy conversation about his business and my job. He assures me that even though we can't prove Dale trashed my apartment, he won't bother me again. Zack won't tell me why he's so sure, but last week Gabriel told me Zack paid Dale a personal visit, which explains why Zack came home with bloody knuckles a month ago. It seems my retired Army Ranger hasn't let becoming rich soften him. If it means I never have to see or hear from Dale again, I'm good with that.

"More coffee?" I ask. Zack shakes his head, and I take our cups and plates to the sink, rinse them, and put them in the dishwasher. His warm breath brushes my neck right before he pulls my earlobe into his mouth and nibbles on it. "Zack, I'm supposed to remind you to show me something."

"You're right. It's nothing outstanding, but I'm going to use it every day."

His words sent threads of heat circling through my stomach and headed south. Now I'm really curious. "Daily, huh?"

"Come with me." Zack takes my hand and leads me upstairs. The door he opens is to a well-fitted exercise room. I see a couple of elliptical machines, a treadmill, a punching bag, and a rack of weights. "I had this installed yesterday while we were at work. You can use this equipment any time you wish."

My heart pounds. The seriousness of his tone sends chills ripping up my spine. "Are you hinting that I need to lose weight?"

"Fuck no. I think you're perfect. But would I enjoy you working out next to me wearing a sports bra and skin-tight shorts? Hell, yes."

"I'm sorry. I misread that."

"Fuck." It's the first time I've seen Zack look bewildered. "I'm not good at this. It's supposed to be an enticement to encourage you to stay."

Very few times in my life have I been speechless. This is one of them. I open my mouth to respond, but nothing comes out. I try to force a few words but all I can manage is to nod in agreement.

"Whoa." Zack laughs. "I didn't mean to scare you." He pulls me into his arms and strokes my back. "You should know by now that I think you're perfect. Come on, I'll show you what else I like to do with my mouth besides sticking my foot in it."

I look up into his eyes and slide my tongue along my lips. "If last night was too rough on you, maybe we should take it easy. You might be too tired to have sex."

His gaze turns stormy and I know he accepts my challenge. "Be careful, you might get more than you wished for."

"I wish for you." I'm getting bolder by the minute, feeling stronger and empowered. I squeal as Zack sweeps me up into his arms, carries me to our bedroom, and carefully stands me in front of his massive bed.

"Strip, fold your clothes, leave them on the chair in the corner, and return to this spot. You will follow my instructions without question. Do not disappoint me, Morgan. If you do, there will be consequences. Do you understand?"

"Yes, Sir." Without another word, I hurriedly undress and do exactly as he says. I take down my hair, shake it loose, and walk back to him.

Zack strokes my hair. "Perfect. Taking down your hair and leaving it loose was the right thing to do."

"Thank you, Sir." Chills streak across my body and my skin grows sensitive as if every single nerve is emitting a strong current of electricity. My heart beats so fast I can hear the blood pulse in my ears. I want Zack. I want him to pleasure me. To make decisions for me. To take charge of me.

"Come here." He extends his hand and I don't hesitate to take it. We walk across the room to a large, dark-wood chest of drawers. "Open the top one."

The dresser has been off-limits to me from day one. On numerous occasions I wanted to snoop, to see what he was hiding, but I didn't. Zack has trusted me in his home, and I didn't want to break that confidence. Now, I'm trembling with anticipation.

The inside of the first drawer is lined in pale blue velvet. My nipples harden at the sight of a variety of vibrators. There's a long thin one, a huge pink one, one that slips over your finger, and a small one with a remote control. A collection of anal toys lay behind them. "Open the second drawer."

I clear my throat and do as instructed. It holds paddles, riding crops, blindfolds, and a host of sexual gadgets in clear boxes. "Have these been here all along?"

"No. I started this collection after we met and have been adding to it."

I lean in closer and inspect some of them. "There are things here I've never heard of, much less seen."

"We'll find the ones that become your favorites."

"You have a mini Club Silken toy stash in your dresser."

His lips brush the soft area between my neck and shoulder. "It's been a long time since I've had a collection." Zack's body is warm behind me. I lean back against him and breathe in his scent. Sandalwood and musk fill my senses.

"That's why everything is still wrapped in cellophane?"

"You deserve the best new toys. Would you like to select a few or do you want me to decide?"

I have no idea what I want. The idea of complete surrender, to trust Zack will never hurt me, makes me strong. "You choose whatever pleases you."

Air whooshes from Zack. "Remember, I will never cause you pain unless you want it." He selects a black, firm but flexible, tapered rubber probe and hands it to me. My heart rate jumps. I know exactly where it goes. I remove the cellophane and hand it back.

"Good." Zack takes a tube of lube and the probe to the bedside table. The soft pop of the lid sends chills up my spine. He reaches his hand out to me. "Come here."

My body is on fire. I'm curious and a little scared as I cross the room to him. He turns me, leans me back against his chest. His hands reach around and lift my breasts as he pushes his rock hard cock against my ass. He nips the vein in my neck and rolls my nipples with his fingers.

"How the fuck did I get so lucky to be at Gloss the night you lost your billfold?" He spins me, his lips crash down on mine. His tongue dives deep into my mouth, as if he intends to explore and lay claim to every inch of me. I don't hesitate to give him everything I have. He finally pulls back and then kisses me tenderly. "I forgot something downstairs. Make yourself comfortable."

He walks out of the room and I snicker at the word. Hot? Needy? Turned on? Yes. But comfortable is not a word to describe how I'm feeling.

The sounds of his footsteps on the stairs send shivers down my bare spine. When he returns, I'm on my knees with them spread shoulder-width apart. My hands are clasped behind my back and my head is inclined forward, my gaze pointing downward. Anticipation floods me and has me so wet, my juices are running down my thighs. I've never experienced this instant flood of moisture until I met Zack. The longing. The ache to have him constantly. I hold my position and wait.

"Morgan, baby." His voice is raspy and barely above a whisper. He kneels in front of me and extends his hands. "Stand."

"Yes, Sir." I rise, push my shoulders back, and offer my breasts to him.

He sets the two bottles of water on the nightstand next to the toy he's selected and then places his hands on my cheeks, lifting my head. I'm lost in the desire in his eyes.

"You're eagerness to please me is overwhelming. Finding you in that position is the sexiest thing I've ever seen." He places my hand on his chest. "Feel that? My heart is about to crack a rib." He places my other hand on the huge erection denied to me by just a few layers of clothing. "That's what you do to me."

"That makes me happy, Sir." If a heart can swell with pride and lust, mine is about to rip out of my chest.

"Get on the bed and move to the middle. You know the position. On your back, with your knees bent, spread wide, and hands at your sides." His tone isn't as raspy as minutes ago, it's strong and demanding.

I can't get there quick enough. My body burns to have him inside of me, slamming as far and hard as possible. The position I'm in allows the cool air to torment my wet pussy. I can feel the moisture flow as he studies me. He's seen every inch of me but I'm no competition for the beautiful women I've seen at Silken. Insecurity dampens my spirit. "Do I please you, Sir?"

"You please me very much." Zack's lips lift into a brilliant smile. He moves to the end of the bed and stares down at my naked body. "You need to come, don't you?"

"Please, Sir."

Zack's brown eyes warm, accompanied by an impish grin. He sits at my feet, leans in, and spreads my outer lips. "Fuck, you're pussy is so beautiful. Show me how you used to pleasure yourself."

"Used to?" I know what he wants and it excites me. God, I'm turning into an exhibitionist.

"You heard me. Starting tomorrow, you won't ever pleasure yourself again unless I permit it." His expression is stoic and I have no doubt he's serious.

"I've never done anything like that before, Sir."

Zack lifts one eyebrow. "Are you saying you've never made yourself come?"

"Never in front of an audience, Sir," I grumble under my breath. Truth be told, I love how he reacts when I push back.

"I am not a fucking 'audience.'" Zack's dark eyes turn ebony.

"No, you're my Dom, Sir."

His brows furrow. "Your position when I reentered this room tells me you know what I expect of you. Yet you challenge me."

Before I can speak I find myself pulled off my back and over his lap. My toes barely touch the floor, my bare ass is pointed at the ceiling, and my fingers dangle down toward the floor. I struggle at first and then stop to look over my shoulder at him. "Sir, are you angry with me?"

His face softens as he gently massages the flesh on my butt. "I will never discipline you in anger. Tell me why you need to be spanked."

I am somewhere between excited, nervous, and a whole lot curious.

Smack. I jump and squeal. A second later, he smacks me even harder. I wiggle, trying to get up. "Are we finished?"

"We're just getting started. Answer the question." Zack holds me in place while his hand strokes my ass cheeks, easing the slight sting. I flinch when two, much harder, slaps land, one on each butt cheek.

I groan. My ass is burning, but endorphins are flowing through my body and the moisture is quickly increasing. Soon Zack's slacks will be wet. I can tell he's enjoying turning my ass pink as much as I am. His cock is hard and pushing into my belly. I know the answer but I don't answer him.

Smack. Smack.

"Mmm," I moan ready to beg. "Again."

"What?" His hands rub against my flesh, easing the burn.

"More please, Sir," I answer quickly.

"You little sneak. You're enjoying this." A rapid burst of slaps wipes everything from my mind. "Spread your knees." His hand slides under me. "If I dip my fingers inside you, will I find you soaking?"

"Yes, Sir."

Zack's fingers slide between the lips of my pussy and they're instantly drenched in my juices. He moans as he turns me over and lifts me onto his lap. His hips rotate under me. "Answer the question and maybe I'll paddle your ass later . . . but only if you're a good girl."

I put the most serious expression I can muster on my face and look him in the eyes. "I'm sorry I failed to follow instructions, Sir." Zack's expression doesn't change. "And I'm sorry I was snarky, Sir."

"That's better." He cups my breasts and pinches my nipples. "I want you in the middle of the bed with your cute ass facing me. Now."

Chapter 10

Zack

My cock jerks at the sight of my handprints on Morgan's ass as she crawls her way to the middle of my bed. She glances over her shoulder and wiggles her butt at me. Fuck. She's going to drive me insane. The memory of her pussy clutching my cock, pulling me deep inside her heat is twisting me in knots. Someday, I'll breach her last virgin hole, but first I'll acquaint her with the beginner's anal plug. I'll be careful stretching Morgan's limits. I'll never push hard enough to break her. Or us.

Morgan turns over onto her back. I stop and stare. "Did I give you permission to do that?"

She gasps and flips back onto her stomach. "I'm sorry, Sir. I wanted to watch you undress."

I sigh. Her face is filled with innocence. "You will learn to respect me. Won't you?"

Morgan's gaze lowers. "Yes, Sir. I will."

"Good. Lesson learned. You may return to your position and watch me."

"Thank you, Sir." Her eyes follow my every move while I finish undressing. I toss my underwear on the floor and stand at the edge of the bed stroking my aching cock. She licks her lips as I strip.

"You approve?"

"I do, Sir. You're a beautiful man, and not just your pretty face. Your body is perfect and that monster cock is gorgeous."

"I'm not sure about the beautiful part but I'm glad you like this." I continue to stroke myself, back and forth. "Show me how you pleasure yourself."

Morgan's hands slowly knead her breasts and her eyes flutter closed. She pinches her nipples, tugging them until they stand hard and red. My plans to have her on her hands and knees shift to the back burner.

"You're so fucking beautiful like that. Relax into it and show me what else pleases you." Slowly, Morgan slides one trembling hand down across her smooth stomach. When her fingers find her clit, her mouth opens and her hips lift. "Open your eyes and look at me."

"Oh, God," she murmurs before locking her blue gaze on me.

I put my hands on her knees. "Spread your legs wider. Let me see all of you." I move closer and slip two fingers into her hot pussy. I find the spot that's sure to make her come.

"Yes. Fuck, yes." Morgan's moans grow in intensity while her fingers work her clit and I pummel her. "I'm going to come. Zack. Please."

"Now. Do it now," I demand. She mumbles words I can't understand as her sweet cunt tightens, clenching and rippling out her orgasm. Her head falls back on the pillows and her hands drop limply to her sides.

Morgan's laugh is low and sexy. "It's never that much fun when I do it alone, Sir."

"I hope not." I join her laughter and move around to stretch out beside her. Her long hair is spread out across the pillow, I swear she's glowing.

"You're quickly becoming my addiction." She sighs and it's the sexiest sound I've ever heard.

"What the fuck is happening to us?" The minute I say it, I want my words back. My question is too deep, too serious, and I don't want to fuck up what we have together.

Morgan rolls to her side and kisses the stubble on my face. "Whatever it is, I hope it never ends."

I reach down and give my cock a few strokes, swirling precum over my fingers.

"May I, Sir," she asked while watching my hand.

"Yes. It pleases me to have your sweet lips wrapped around my cock." She replaces my hand with hers and my dick twitches at her touch. I roll over on my back, slide a pillow under my head, and watch. She slides down my body, kissing and licking my skin. Her gaze never leaves mine. When her warm, wet tongue laps at the head of my cock like a kitten given a warm bowl of cream, I almost lose it. "Take all of me."

I let out a breath and force myself not to lose control when she opens her mouth and sucks me deep inside. Pulling back, her tongue plays with my slit, sliding around it to lick that sensitive spot right under the head. Morgan's eyes are full of lust as she pulls me to the back of her throat again, and I feel her reflex to gag. God, I'm on the edge, ready to empty myself into her sweet mouth and let her swallow everything I give her, but I hold back. We aren't finished until she comes on my cock with the plug in her ass. She pulls back to take a breath and my hands tighten on her jaws.

Still holding me in her hand she lifts her head. Lust-glazed, blue eyes look at me in question. "Is something wrong, Sir?"

"If it was any more right, I would have come in your mouth."

Morgan sticks out her tongue and licks the tip of my dick. It twitches in approval, and my heart clutches as if something has it in a vise. "And how is that a bad thing, Sir?" she asks sweetly.

"I'm going to be inside you when I come." I move to the side of the bed and grab the lube and toy. "On your hands and knees. Head down with your hot little ass pointed at me exactly as I wanted before we were sidetracked."

"That completely slipped my mind." Her cheeks are glowing, and I let the fact she failed to say Sir slide this time. Morgan is in position in record time.

"You are my brave girl." I open the lube and move closer, letting a few drops fall between her cheeks. "Morgan, reach back and hold your cheeks open."

I run my fingers through her moisture and then use that and the lube to rub circles around her tiny opening. Her heavy moan tells me she's getting into this, so I insert one finger to the first joint and make small circles inside her. Then add a second, spreading my fingers, hoping I don't come from just watching.

Morgan pushes back into me. "More, please, Sir."

My God, the woman is fucking perfect. I remove my fingers, coat the toy with lube, and slide the small end inside her. "Relax and don't fight me. Push against it."

"Like this?"

"Yes, baby. Exactly like that." I add another drop of oil and push deeper until the plug is seated perfectly. "Color?"

"Green, Sir. Please, I need you."

I position my knees behind her, slide a couple of inches of my dick inside her pussy, and let her adjust to the pressure of having the plug and my cock inside her at the same time. Morgan has to want this or it ends immediately.

She pushes herself back trying to force more of me inside her. I grab her hips and slowly apply pressure. Watching as my cock slides deeper into her tight pussy with the large base of the plug in place is beyond amazing. "You're so fucking tight this way." I pull my eyes away and look at the ceiling as I bury myself to the hilt.

"Oh, God. The sensation is incredible. Please, Sir." She's squirming and panting. "Move. Fuck me."

I give her what she needs and pound into her as fast and hard as I can, building the momentum until we fall into a frenzied rhythm. My balls tighten, ready to empty into her, but I wait. Her soft cries of pleasure tell me she's close, so I lean over her back and slide my finger through her moisture to her clit. She tightens around me and her moans grow louder. I pinch her tiny bud.

"Come now," I demand. Morgan's pussy clenches me, clamping down again and again. I push deeper into her, grinding my cock against her walls, and I don't let up until her body relaxes with a small shiver.

"Fuuuck." I let myself go, pounding into her until my cock is shooting strings of cum, and I'm ready to collapse. I remove the plug and place it on the bedside table then roll over, holding onto her so we're on our sides spooned. She twists her shoulder so she can turn her head toward me. She looks into my eyes and smiles. Suddenly, I can't imagine life without her. "I'm so damn proud of your willingness to try new things."

"You are wonderful. That was wonderful. I can't wait to feel every inch of you, hard and hot inside my body."

"I will never stop wanting you." I barely prevent myself from saying more. There's still time to decide about our future, but I know what I hope it will be. "We made a mess. Lie still. I'll clean you up."

Morgan smiles at me. "I don't mind. We made it together."

"Yes, we did." I go to the bathroom, grab a cloth out of the cabinet, and hold it under the water until it's warm. She's still on her side when I lower myself to the bed. "Rollover."

"Yes, Sir." Morgan's chest, neck, and cheeks are still flushed from her orgasm.

"Spread your legs." She quickly does what I asked. "Watching my cum trickle out of your pussy is a beautiful thing."

"Truth or lie?"

"Oh, truth. Definitely truth." Her eyes close while I wash her. She looks happy, almost angelic. I throw the washcloth in the laundry bin and return to brush the hair off her face. "Hmm, if we play our cards right we can do this a couple of times more today."

Morgan lifts onto her elbow and looks at her cell. "That's once after brunch. We can probably squeeze one more in before dinner."

Laughter rolls out of me. I feel lighter, happier with her in my life. "I'll do my best not to disappoint."

"You didn't realize you were creating a monster, did you?"

"I'm very fond of monsters." I turn her onto her back, lean down and rest my forehead against hers. "It's still early enough for you to rest while I attend to a little business. Is that all right? There's plenty of time between now and going to the club around nine."

"May I invite Kayla to the club?"

"If you like. You're not inviting Chelsea?"

"I don't know if she's interested in going, but it won't hurt to ask." A memory of Kayla quizzing me about Silken flashes though my mind. "Kayla has mentioned it more than once.

"It's up to you. Nick will be at the club tonight. I don't know about Slider, but both of them are allowing the managers of Gloss and Gallants to take on more responsibility. It's time for us to trust that we've made the right choices in who can run the three clubs."

"Didn't you call Nick the whore-dog of the group?"

"That's Slider, but I might have exaggerated a little. Not to say Nick or Slider are saints, but Slider's more of a one-time hit with the ladies. He's cautious about long-term relationships. There's a story there. It's just not mine to tell."

Morgan is sitting on the edge of the bed. Her eyes are sparkling as she all but leaps into my arms. I catch her mid-air and wrap her legs around my waist just as she throws her arms around my neck and squeals in my ear. "Thank you. I wasn't sure if I should ask to bring them or not."

"I'll think of a way you can reward me, and, right now, your naked body pressed against mine is giving me lots of ideas." I inhale, taking in her scent. Citrus shampoo and the scent of sex has my dick twitching. "You can ask me for anything, you know that, right?"

Morgan smiles. "I do now. I'll contact Kayla and Chels while you're working."

Reluctantly, I release Morgan and slide on a pair of warm-ups. "Are you going back to bed?"

"Not until I talk with the girls."

"I won't be tied up long. We have shopping to do." I lift an eyebrow to stop Morgan from arguing. "Don't deny me the pleasure of buying you things. Tell your friend a driver will be at the apartment at nine to pick her up."

****

Morgan

I slip on shorts and a T-shirt and call Chels first. She deserves the chance to accept or refuse the invitation. She answers on the first ring.

"Hey. I wondered if I'd hear from you this weekend."

"I have good news," I say, but before I can ask her anything, she squeals as if I've stuck her with a knife.

"Zack proposed! I had a gut feeling. Monday, we'll start planning an engagement party."

"Stop." I'm laughing at her leap of logic and tell her the real reason I'm calling. "Nobody proposed anything except for an invitation for you and Kayla to go to Silken tonight."

She doesn't even think about it before she blurts out, "Thanks, but I'm not interested. I'm on my way to the airport to see my brother. He's flying back to base but has a layover until late tonight."

"Maybe next time." Chels and her brother are close despite the four year age difference.

"Kayla's going be one happy bitch. She's planning on fixing popcorn and watching a movie tonight." Chels voice doesn't sound quite as tense as before.

"Tell your brother I said hello, okay?"

I end the call and reach out to Kayla, hoping she'll be more comfortable knowing the night is all hers. Our call doesn't last but a minute.

"Ohmygod, ohmygod!" She exclaims. "I've been dying to go to The Special Touch to buy a sexy outfit." Her excitement is palpable and infectious. "I can't wait to see what goes on at Silken."

I give her the phone number to call the shop for an appointment and then head to the shower. I'm excited yet nervous to share my new lifestyle with one of my best friends. After I disconnect the call, I stretch out on the bed to relax, but the sheets smell like Zack and sex. My brain refuses to rest. Soon I admit to myself it isn't happening, so I get up, take my shower, and try on a few different outfits for tonight. I finally slip on a pair of skinny jeans, a lightweight pale blue sweater, and my favorite ankle boots. Now that I'm ready for my shopping excursion, I go downstairs to make coffee and feed Zack a healthy snack.

Zack hasn't been in his office for a long time but I fix a cup of coffee and carry it to him with a plate of fruit, granola, and yogurt. He's in front of his computer, gazing intently at the screen, which is all charts and graphs.

I stop at the door. "Knock, knock."

"Is that for me?" He turns toward me and his serious expression vanishes. "Didn't we recently eat?"

"Two muffins aren't a lot of food, besides, I was getting lonely."

"Bring it here." His deep timbre vibrates through my clit.

I drop my gaze to the floor and take him his coffee. "I hope it pleases you, Sir."

"You please me." He looks down at the plate in front of him and then up at me. A grimace darkens his face. "Yogurt and granola? You expect me to eat this?"

He doesn't scare me with that look. I roll my eyes. "I added a couple of things to the grocery list. I'm trying to keep you healthy."

Zack shakes his head. "Thanks. I think. What's the word on the girls?"

"Chels already has plans but Kayla is thrilled. She's calling The Special Touch for an appointment."

"Good. I'll call and have her clothes put on our bill."

"Zack. I hadn't thought of the expense. She doesn't earn a lot of money in the payroll department." My heart swells like a balloon. I almost blurt out that I love him but I don't.

"Go. I have maybe an hour left here."

I turn and start to leave the room. "Wait. Did you say our bill?"

"I told you we're going shopping." He smiles at me patiently. "I heard The Special Touch has a shipment of new dresses." He winks at me and my insides quiver.

****

Morgan

Zack and I sit in one of the booths at the front of the club, keeping an eye out for Kayla. Nick brings our drinks and sits next to me where he can see the door as well. He seems to be fairly anxious to meet Kayla.

"So it's after nine, do you think your friend backed out?"

"Not Kayla, she's the adventurous one of the group." I check my phone but have no messages from her. "If something had happened, she would have left me a message.

"And I would have heard from the driver. I'll find out." Zack taps Gabriel's number into the cell. After a short conversation, he's chuckling when he ends the call. "She's already here."

"Where? We've been watching the door." Nick stands and looks around.

A woman sitting at the far end of the bar wearing a red lace mask and a skin-colored spandex dress raises her drink and toasts us. She stands and walks in our direction. Every male at the bar is watching her hips sway.

"Oh, my God!" I start to push Zack out of the booth but freeze. "Sir, may I go to her?"

He lifts my chin. "Yes, of course."

Kayla's smile tells me she's already having a good time. I grab her and hug her. "I was feeling uneasy about you."

"I'm sorry. I wanted a few minutes to be completely anonymous."

"You're here now and you're stunning. I didn't even realize that was you."

"I put my hair up so it wouldn't give me away." She turns in a circle. "What do you think?" The dress hugs every inch of her body. And her legs look like they run on for miles.

"I think every man here has a hard-on for you, including Zack. Kayla, you can pick and choose. Just watch the color of their armband."

"Where's your ribbon?"

I touch the diamond choker around my neck. It's the approved substitute for the ribbon. "Zack bought it for me today. Isn't it beautiful?"

"It's stunning. Don't let me forget to thank him for my clothes."

"Did you sign your guest papers?"

"Yes. Gabriel explained the rules and had me sign them. I can't afford a membership, that's for damn sure."

"Relax, you're here as a guest and you're safe."

"I'll make sure she doesn't get into trouble." Nick steps to Kayla's side. "Nicholas, better known to my friends as Nick." He extends his hand and she takes it. Neither of them appears to be in a hurry to release the other.

"Kayla." She's almost purring just looking at Nick. "I hear you're a favorite with the ladies." I catch her quick glance at his crotch and sure enough, the ridge behind the zipper in his slacks is obvious.

"I probably can't live up to what you've heard, but I'll try." Nick's smile is downright menacing. "Would you like to join Morgan and Zack, or may I show you around first?"

"I haven't been any farther than the bar so I'd love a tour." Kayla, my amazingly forward friend, isn't holding back tonight. She slips her hand around Nick's bicep and turns toward me. "Don't wait up, Mom."

I stand there with my mouth open as Nick, smiling like a cat high on catnip, walks away with Kayla on his arm. Somehow, I sense Zack's presence behind me. It could be his cologne, but I think my body is so in tune with his it knows before I do.

"She'll be fine. Nick will follow the club rules just like I did with you. Nothing will happen unless she wants it to." He moves my hair to the side and slides his tongue up the vein in my neck. He nips me before wrapping his arms around my waist. "And since they're now occupied, I have plans for you."

"Hmm, sounds interesting. What do you have in mind?"

"I reserved a room."

"You're just full of good ideas. What do you have planned, Sir?" I sway against him, feeling him harden as my ass rubs him. He takes my hand and leads me to a scene room.

"Do you remember me asking if you'd like two men taking you at the same time?"

I nod, not sure I'm ready to take that step. "If it pleases you, Sir."

We walk inside the room and Zack closes the door and throws the lock. Before I know it, I'm against the wall and he's devouring my mouth. He pulls back, his knuckles grazing down my cheeks. "It doesn't please me and it's not going to happen in the foreseeable future. This body is mine."

He was testing me? Or teasing? I don't care. He doesn't want to share me and that thrills me to my core. I want so badly to tell him how much he means to me, but I push my emotions aside and enjoy his body pressed against mine. "Sir, may I speak freely while in the room?"

He studies me for a minute and then his face softens. "Yes. Undress and sit on the table."

He doesn't have to tell me to fold my clothes and place them on the chair. I do it because that's the way he wants it and making him happy pleases me. The padded table is cool on my bare skin.

He strips quickly, and I can't help but watch. His body is a work of art. "Lay back. There, that's fine." Zack runs his hands all over me, lighting fires under my skin along the way. It's a light touch, and my body gets hotter from the inside out. Anticipation makes me wetter by the minute.

"Hmm. I love your hands, Sir."

"Just my hands?" His thumb and forefinger pinch my nipples into hard buds.

"I have great affection for your cock too, Sir." Zack chuckles. I love the sound. It's in harmony with my soul.

"I like hearing my brave girl talking dirty. Coming from your mouth that one word makes me hard as stone. Are you brave enough to try the next size anal trainer?"

"Absolutely." I'm comfortable with anything Zack chooses. He's proven again and again he will never hurt me. He turns and opens a drawer. The sound of a package opening excites me and I hold my breath until he holds it up for me to see. "That's the next size?"

"It is. Remember, it's your call. We can stick with the smaller plug if you want." His face is void of expression, not putting any pressure on me at all.

This process will make it easier for me to have anal sex with Zack. I want what he wants. "No. I choose the one in your hand."

His lips crash down on mine taking my breath away. "I'll make it good for you."

I want to please him and I trust him with all my heart. "I know."

"Get on your hands and knees." He helps me turn over and when I'm in position, he spreads my knees wide. "Fuck you're beautiful."

I groan loudly as he separates my lips and his tongue laps at the moisture between my legs. His fingers press down on my clit while his tongue is deep inside me. He pulls away from me and I cry out. "I'm so close, Sir."

"No," he insists. "I'll tell you when to come."

I hear the snap of a lid that I know belongs to a bottle of lube. A couple of drops of cool oil fall on my anus. Zack rubs in circles, slowly inserting one finger and then two, sliding them in and out, stretching me. "Feel good?"

"God, yes."

"Put your face down flat on the table and hold your cheeks open for me."

I move into position with my head down and my body braced on my shoulders. I'm turned on as hell, yet nervous too. If he touches my clit again, I may explode without permission.

Zack's fingers leave me, and I turn my head to watch as he soaks the plug with lube. The cool rubber presses against my ass. "Remember to breathe and push against the pressure. It will help loosen your outer ring." He leans down and kisses the small of my back and pushes the head of the plug inside me.

"Oh, God." It stings slightly and he lets me rest for a minute, reaching under me to stroke my clit. It distracts me enough that the plug slides inside me. Zack massages my cheeks and I move my hands back to the table.

"I wish you could see how fucking sexy you are."

The pressure inside me is exquisite, but I need more. Much more.

"Damn it, Sir. Fuck me, please." I'm surprised when the table slowly lowers, but when I feel Zack standing close behind me I understand. I'm just at the right level for him to slide inside me.

"With pleasure." His cock rubs back and forth until the tip is nudging my clit, stimulating me beyond all thought as I moan and pant with desire. Finally, with one thrust from behind, he's deep inside me.

"Yes," I whimper. "I'm so full with you inside me, Sir . . . oh, God, it feels so good." I push back taking him as deep as possible.

"Fuck, you feel like heaven. I belong here. Belong inside you. Belong to you."

Words cease as we fall into the give and take of two people whose bodies crave each other. He does belong inside me. I'm his home.

"Harder, Sir. Harder," I plead loudly, and he obliges by pounding into me so hard he has to grip my hips to keep me on the table. The waves are building, getting larger with each thrust as his pubic bone pounds the plug in my ass, and his cock stretches my walls. He reaches between us and works my clit.

"Come," he demands. "Come now."

My body crashes into the deep abyss.

Zack roars and empties jets of cum inside me. With each spray my orgasm strengthens, giving me more and more pleasure. Breathing hard, he turns me onto my back and kisses my lips, cheek, and then neck. His lips are soft and his touch is tender as he whispers something against my skin I don't understand. Or do I?

The intensity of my orgasm releases me in a slow fall back to earth.

I wake wrapped in a blanket with Zack holding me in his arms. The first thing I notice is the most beautiful expression on his face. The second is that the plug is gone. "You dominate me in a very good way. We're amazing together, Sir."

Zack holds a bottle of water to my lips and I drink half of it. I like that we're away from the customers and in the area reserved for the owners. The light is dim and the sound from the rest of the club seems far away. "Together is the operative word."

I snuggle my face in the curve of his neck. We sit silently, lost in our own thoughts for a long time. *Wait. Did he tell me he loved me or was that a dream? Was it wishful thinking?* I'm afraid to ask. Afraid if I say I love him, I'll lose him, I whisper, "Zack?"

"Hmm?"

"Never mind." I burrow my face deeper into his neck.

He shifts me so I'm in the crook of his arm, facing him. "Never mind doesn't work. We tell each other the truth."

I study his new expression. He looks so happy, so at peace. "Did you say . . .?" I can't finish my question. What if I'm wrong?

"Yes, I love you," he says without hesitation.

His smile brings tears to my eyes. "I love you too."

"Truth or lie?" He raises one eyebrow.

"Truth. I swear." I sink against him. He loves me. Zack Pierce loves me. My heart is so full I can't stop the tears from sliding down my cheeks.

"Those better be tears of happiness. I never want to see you cry for any other reason."

I cover his face and neck with kisses. "Yes, Sir."

"I never thought I'd say those words again. Now, all I want to do is shout them."

"Feel free to say it again and again. I'll never tire of hearing you tell me that you love me." Zack sighs a sound of relief. We stayed where we were for a long time, neither of us speaking, just occasionally looking at each other with love, pride, and happiness.

"Zack?"

"Hmm?"

I hate to interrupt our moment. "I need to visit the restroom."

His chest moves under my cheek with his chuckle. "Whatever you need."

Still wrapped securely, he carries me to the scene room for my clothes and waits while I dress. We stroll to the restroom, stopping occasionally to kiss and grin like two people in love.

After I've done my best to repair my hair, I splash water on my face and get dressed. I push open the restroom door and find him standing right where I left him.

"You waited for me." I leaned forward and kissed his neck.

"Always." He wraps his arm around my waist, dropping his hands to rest on my hip and we walk back to our booth up front.

I pause and look around. "Do you see Kayla or Nick?"

"No, but then I haven't looked. I'll find out what they're up too." Zack walks over and speaks with the bartender. Then he fishes his cell from his pocket and makes a call.

I dial her number, sure she'll pick up. I'll be surprised if she's in a scene room with Nick since they just met, but it's possible. I walk to the bar and stand beside Zack, waiting until he ends the call.

"Kayla and Nick returned to the bar after their tour. She spoke to someone on the phone, went out the front door, and never came back." Zack's shoulder's lift. "She told Gabriel she had a family emergency and needed a ride home. Taylor drove her."

My heart squeezes. "I don't think she has family here in Chicago." I dial her number again and beg her to call me.

Nick walks out of the office cond Zack and I meet him halfway. "What did Kayla say to you?"

He looked at me then Zack and shrugged. "Absolutely nothing."

Zack slid his hand around my waist. "Tell us what happened."

"I took her on a tour. She seemed interested and was asking a lot of questions. We were watching a caning scene when she excused herself to go to the restroom. When she didn't return I looked for her until Gabriel told me she'd left."

"I'll call Chels." Zack stands next to me while I wait for her to answer.

"Tell her if she hears from Kayla, we're ready to provide any help she needs."

"Thank you." How I got so lucky to meet Zack will forever be a mystery but I'm so glad I did.

After a few words with Chels, I disconnect, feeling a little better. "Chels spoke with Kayla. All she said was she had to go home for a while. She asked Chels to let work know."

"Where's home?

"Northern Arkansas, I think. She never talks about her past."

"Family emergency makes sense. If there's a crisis, Kayla probably didn't think to tell you she was leaving."

"I hope you're right."

"Are you ready to go home?"

A slow smile spreads across my face. "I like the sound of that. Home."

After we tell Nick goodbye, we stop and let Gabriel know we're leaving. He's thumbing through a stack of papers. Zack claps him on the shoulder. "See you."

"Have a good evening."

"You, too." Zack holds my hand as we walk outside.

I stop and look up at the sky. "It's a beautiful night."

"Out here, away from the city lights, you can see so many more stars."

"I have a question."

Zack stops and looks at me. "Shoot."

"Why the name Club Silken?"

I squeal when he picks me up, pushes my dress up, and then sits me on the hood of his car. "Zack, somebody may come outside."

"Let 'em." He snaps my breakaway thong apart and dives face-first between my legs. He laps at me like he's starving and I'm his only nourishment.

I clamp my mouth shut to keep from making so much noise somebody might hear and rush outside. I'm still tender but within seconds I'm coming on his tongue. After I stop thrashing, he snaps my panties and then helps me to the ground.

I laugh at the audacity of this man I love with all my heart. "That was amazing, but you didn't answer my question."

"Because there's nothing better than the silky, soft skin of a woman's pussy."

I shake my head and laugh. "You mean *my* pussy, don't you, Sir?"

"Only your pussy."

Epilogue

Six months later

Morgan

Sweat pools at the base of my spine. I turn over on my back, open my eyes, and find the sexiest man alive standing over me. He hands me a frozen daiquiri. "You are too good to me." I take a sip letting the cold liquid slide down my throat. "Thanks. I needed that."

Zack stretches out in the chair next to me and removes his sunglasses. "Are you having a good time?"

"Yes. A wonderful time. It's beautiful here. The water is so clear, I can be chest deep and still see the color of my toenail polish. The climate is perfect."

"Judging by the color of your skin, you need a little more sunblock."

I glance at my bare breasts. "You know anybody who'd be willing to help me out?" I pick up the bottle of lotion from the side table and hold it up.

"Any number of men on the beach would be happy to assist you." Zack's lips lift into a sly smile. "Interested?"

I tap my lips with my finger. "Hmm. You know who gets my vote for the best hands."

He takes the lotion and squeezes a glob right between my breasts, the cool lotion makes me jump and my nipples tighten. Then he moves to sit on the edge of my lounge chair and his hands hover over my nipples. "I'm not so sure about that, you were really into watching the threesome last night."

I take his hands and smear them through the lotion and over my breasts. "It was nice having the extra stimulation, but I prefer you."

His hands are warm and strong as he rubs my nipples, making them stand erect and desperate for more of his touch. I flinch when he tightens his grip.

"I'm sorry. Are you sensitive from the clamps?"

I squirm in my chair, remembering the rush of blood to my nipples when the clamps came off. "A little, but not enough to complain."

"You never complain."

I notice a pretty woman watching Zack. I catch her eye and wink. "You have an admirer."

"She's too late. We're leaving for home tomorrow, and tonight I'm keeping you to all to myself."

I slide over, turn on my side, and pat the empty space. "Squeeze in here with me."

"My pleasure. I like it when you're slippery." Zack wedges in next to me and pulls my legs over his.

We're silent while we watch the smattering of white clouds, the clear blue sky, and the water sparkling under the sun's rays. Couples are spread out across the beach in various stages of undress. A few are indulging in sex under the sun. Apparently, there are members-only clubs all over the world and Zack found this one on a privately owned island for our special week. Admission is by invitation only. The resort is plush and the club is decorated with expensive furnishings.

His hand slowly works its way to the edge of my bikini bottoms. "I'm happy you've had a good time."

"It's the best engagement present I've ever had." I slip my fingers inside his bathing suit.

"It's the first and last engagement gift you'll ever get." He laughs while tugging at the tie at my hip.

I lift onto my elbow, wrap my hand around his rock hard cock, and pin him with my gaze. "Truth or lie?"

He dips his finger inside my wet pussy. "Truth."

Unedited excerpt from Come Hot
Kayla

The soft click of the exit door closing, reminds me the weekly sessions with Dr. Meeks are over. For almost five months, I've regurgitated every detail of my past and present. We've dug into and explored places in my mind my subconscious had long buried.

Today is the first time my insides don't feel like they've been strung out and picked apart by hungry wolves.

I should be happy not to be the flippant woman I used to be.

I should be happy to shed daylight on the secrets I used to hide.

I should be happy to be myself, Kayla Jean Britton.

What I am is scared of the future.

I give my parking ticket to the valet, take my phone from my purse, and stare at it. There are two calls I need to make but I'm not sure how to start the conversation. I'm determined to repair my friendship with Chels Coffman and Morgan Kimball or at least try. Truth be told, I miss them.

How will I be received? Will they talk to me? Want to see me? My car rolls up and stops. The valet exits, holding the door for me. I tip him and drive away. I breathe easier because I'm in heavy traffic and temporarily relieved of making any calls.

Last year at this time, I could've knocked on either of their doors and been welcome. All I can hope for now is they don't turn away from me.

Chels and Morgan were my best friends and coworkers before I bolted from Club Silken and disappeared.

I miss them dearly and hope they welcome me back.

Chapter 1

Kayla

The parking lot at the apartment complex looks the same, well, except there's a vehicle under the carport in slot four-eighty-three. It used to be mine. I park in one of the visitor's spots, turn off the key, and sit in silence.

Wednesday used to be Chinese food night for Morgan Kimball, Chelsea Coffman and me. We all lived in the same complex so meeting at Chels' place was easy. We'd order in and eat ourselves into a state of bliss. Morgan might be living with Zack Pierce, and it's possible Chels has moved, but I have to take a chance.

I get out of my car, stuff the keys in my purse, and start down the sidewalk. My heart is pounding, my palms are sweating, and my nerves are just about frazzled when a high-pitched squeal startles the crap out of me. I look toward the sound.

"Kayla," Chels cries out. "Oh. My. God. It's really you."

My chest hurts as I brace myself to catch the woman running toward me. She doesn't slow down until her arms are wrapped around me. We stumble but together we regain our footing. Tears flood my eyes and run down my cheeks. I'm so relieved at my reception my knees are weak and the knot in my throat prevents me from speaking.

Chels speaks instead. "Thank, God. We've been worried about you."

"I'm sorry," I manage to say. I hold her away from me so I can look at her. "It's so good to see you."

She takes my hand and gives me a stern expression, which makes me smile. "Well, you're not getting away from me. Come on. It's Wednesday and we're ordering Chinese, opening a bottle of wine, and then you're telling me what the hell happened to make you rush home." She frowns as she glances at her cell. "Club Silken isn't open on Wednesdays; I'll bet she's free tonight."

"How is she?"

"She and Zack Pierce are engaged and she's beyond happy."

"I'm glad. I hate that embarrassed her."

"Why would you think that?"

"She and Zack invited me to the club and right in the middle of the evening I left and disappeared."

"She's not upset about that. I told them there was a problem and you had to rush home to Arkansas. Is she worried about you? Hell yes. You never returned any of our calls or messages. We should call her."

I stop in my tracks. I'm not sure I'm ready for one of our girl's nights. "Please, don't." I take a deep breath. "I'd like to spend a few hours with you."

Chels eyes are full of questions but she smiles. "Whatever you want."

"I'll reach out to Morgan tomorrow."

"I hope you do. I think she's been waiting for you to return."

"Waiting? For me?" Guilt builds in my stomach and I question the wisdom of eating Chinese.

Chels loops her arm in mine and we walk to her apartment. "She wants us both in her wedding. You have to call her."

"When is the wedding?"

"Rehearsal is this Friday and the wedding is Monday."

"That's tomorrow. Maybe I should wait until after the wedding."

"Stop. That would break her heart."

"Will Zack's friend, Nick, be there?" Maybe if I pretend I don't remember much about him I can hide my embarrassment. He'd taken me on a tour of Zack Pierce's members only club. Nick's hands were large and warm around my waist. The connection had been immediate or it had been for me. One scene triggered memories of being lashed with a leather belt across my back to the point of leaving whelps and I freaked. The night just got worse when my brother called and I went racing from the building.

"I'm sure he will."

"I don't know if I'm ready to see Nick."

"He probably doesn't remember it. So what if he does?"

Tears build in the back of my eyes. I'm so grateful that they're welcoming me back. I feel more like I'm returning to family with Chels than I did at home. I'll share my past or at least part of it with her.

About the Author

A student of creative writing in her youth, Jerrie set aside her passion when life presented her with a John Wayne husband and a wonderful daughter. Her love for romantic suspense inspires her to write alpha males and kick-ass women. Her characters weave their way through death and danger to emerge stronger, because of, and on occasion, in spite of, their love for each other. If they're tough enough, they live happily ever after.

Jerrie lives in Texas, denies having an accent, thrives on sunshine, children's laughter, sugar (human and granulated), and researching for her heroes and heroines. She loves to hear from her readers. Find a complete list of her books at http://www.jerriealexander.com or contact her at jerrie@jerriealexander.com.

Read more at www.jerriealexander.com.